'In my opinion, the position of secretary is too often confused with that of nursemaid or mother, and I can assure you, Pam, that my feelings for Mr Carmichael are not in the least maternal!'

'And I can assure *you*, Miss Phillipson, that I would be extremely disappointed if they were!'

Pamela gasped as Tamar felt the hot tide of embarrassment flood her cheeks with colour.

Unheard by either girl, Dagan Carmichael had emerged from his den to stand in the communicating doorway, one hand resting over his head on the lintel, the other pressed into the small of his back, as if he was stretching his tired muscles. He looked big and tough and awe-inspiring.

Tamar clenched her jaw. She wouldn't apologise. She just wouldn't. Her remark had been ill-timed and she regretted he'd overheard it, but in itself it was nothing but the truth.

RASH
INTRUDER

BY
ANGELA WELLS

MILLS & BOON LIMITED
ETON HOUSE   18-24 PARADISE ROAD
RICHMOND   SURREY   TW9 1SR

First published in Great Britain 1989
by Mills & Boon Limited

© Angela Wells 1989

Australian copyright 1989

ISBN 0 263 12210 7

Set in Times Roman 10 on 11¾ pt.
07-8910-56571 C

Made and printed in Great Britain

CHAPTER ONE

TAMAR paid off the taxi, and with a sigh lifted her heavy suitcase. At the time it had seemed a wonderful idea to spend the very last moment possible swimming in the Aegean Sea. If she'd known her flight from Athens would be forced to make an unscheduled landing at Munich for technical reasons and she was going to be delayed by several hours, she certainly wouldn't have chosen to travel back to London wearing only jeans and a thin cotton blouse over her bikini!

Dragging her suitcase up the short flight of steps, she entered the vast Intercontinental Newspress Incorporated building, thankful that like most daily newspaper publishing houses its doors were open twenty-four hours a day.

There was one consolation at least. One of the advantages of being senior secretary to the group advertisement director was that she could use his private bathroom when he wasn't there—and Hugh Drummond certainly wouldn't be there at seven-thirty in the morning. Going by past form, he was unlikely to put in an appearance before ten, or even later, since this would be his first day back from holiday too. She smiled sourly to herself. One of the disadvantages of working for Hugh was that he always insisted she fit her holidays in with his own, so that in their joint absence all business was handled by his deputy, and Hugh didn't have to make do with a temp. when she took her own annual leave.

Shouldering her way awkwardly through the heavy glass doors, she caught sight of her reflection and grimaced. Good grief, what a sight she looked in her casual clothes, with her normally smooth blonde hair scraped up in an untidy ponytail! Originally she'd planned to return to her flat first, but the flight delay had made that impossible. Still, a quick shower, clean undies from her suitcase and a change into the linen suit she kept for emergencies in the office wardrobe, and she would feel as good as new, she told herself—or as near to that as possible, seeing she hadn't had much sleep in the past twenty-four hours.

Her security pass was still at home, but since she had worked for INI for six years—ever since leaving her first, shortlived job on a rival newspaper—her identity was unlikely to be challenged.

'Good holiday, Miss Phillipson?' The young man behind the reception desk cast frankly approving eyes at her. Aware that the blue bikini top was sharply visible through her thin cotton blouse and appeared to form a focus for his impertinent eyes, Tamar took the proffered office keys from his hands quickly.

'Very good, thank you, Frank,' she told him tersely.

In the bright light of Greece her outfit had been infinitely becoming. In London on a cool September morning it seemed merely provocative, and she wanted to change into something more suitable without delay.

'Go with the boyfriend, did you?'

Tamar smiled tightly, not deigning to reply, conscious that the youth's gaze lingered on her slim, curvaceous hips in the tight jeans as she stooped to lift the case. Just like all men, she thought resignedly. He probably even thought she would be flattered by his obvious admiration. She would have been better pleased if he'd given her a hand with her luggage!

As the lift sped towards the eighth floor, she stared moodily at the emergency phone on the wall. It was almost as if there was a conspiracy afoot to delve into her private life. In the fast-living, high-excitement environment of a newspaper office, to be twenty-four, unmarried, unengaged and not officially involved with a man seemed to make her a freak.

Even her young assistant Pamela regarded her with a kind of pity, which was infuriating, particularly as Pamela's relationships seemed to bring her more pain than pleasure, if one measured the amount of time she spent sobbing into the filing.

Supposing she *had* accepted Neil's invitation to spend her summer holiday with him at his parents' timeshare apartment in Spain? That would have set the tongues wagging! For months the young account executive had been trying to turn their friendship into something deeper. But in her heart she'd known the prospect was never on, even without her lack of freedom to fix her own holiday dates.

The truth was, she had learned a painful and humiliating lesson at eighteen, one that still coloured her reaction to the casual affairs she saw taking place around her every day. Her contemporaries might think her strange, but she knew that she would need to give her heart first before she gave her body—and, pleasant though Neil was, she wasn't in love with him.

Fortunately the lifts were close to her office, as her suitcase seemed to be growing heavier by the second. Letting it thump down on the floor, she put her key into the lock of the outer office—and froze.

The door was already unlocked. If Pamela had forgotten to lock it last Friday, Security would have remedied the omission when they did their rounds. If the cleaners were in, she would have seen or heard them.

Cautiously she pushed the door open, entering the first of the four offices which comprised the directors' suite. This was Pamela's office—a small, pleasant room with all the usual office equipment where the day-to-day filing was kept. A quick glance showed all the expensive electronic equipment was still in place, and breathing a tentative sigh of relief Tamar moved towards the connecting door to her own much larger room.

Here all the confidential filing was kept in locked cabinets: detailed statistics, outlines of deals being offered to advertising agencies in efforts to bring in more revenue for INI, survey reports gained at great expense and used as bargaining power, sometimes with agents, sometimes direct with clients. In the game of bluff they played with other newspaper houses in the fight to get advertising revenue, the information in these cabinets played a vital part.

It was with a sinking feeling in her stomach that Tamar discovered the door to her office was also unlocked, her heart beating a tattoo as she observed that one drawer of the filing-cabinet was pulled open and was devoid of contents.

Oh, lord! This was all she needed—industrial espionage on her first day back! With an angry gesture of despair, she put her knee to the empty drawer, sending it spinning back into place with a clang that made the entire cabinet shudder as she reached out to ring Security; but before her hand could make contact with the receiver the far door connecting her own office with Hugh Drummond's was suddenly flung open. Her hand suspended over the phone, she shrieked out her shock. Fool that she was, she hadn't given a thought to the intruder still being on the premises. Now she was caught entirely at his mercy, her grey eyes widening in apprehension as she stared back at him.

Her first impression was of height. He must be every inch of six feet two, she thought. At five feet six, and nine stone, Tamar herself was no delicate blossom, and she registered faintly that it must be the width of his shoulders that gave her such an instant impression of power, making her feel fragile by contrast.

Eyes as darkly blue as the recently left Aegean slid over her from top to toe, taking their time, assessing her from beneath thick, straight brows as dark as a starless night.

He didn't look like an industrial spy. That was, if you expected someone thin, shabby and rather furtive-looking. On the contrary, the glistening grey material of his close-fitting trousers obviously owed their gleam to expensive fabric rather than overwear, and the white shirt with its thin grey stripe and neatly folded-back sleeves had never been bought from a chain-store. Hair that thick also had to have been styled at some expense to give such a well-groomed appearance to a face that could have belonged to a buccaneer in an earlier age—tough, uncompromising and with a daredevil tilt to the square jaw with its strongly rounded chin.

Also, if he'd been caught in a nefarious act, he should be looking guilty. Instead he merely looked irritated and impatient. After that first daunting, travelling stare which had rooted her to the spot, he gave her a brief, super-ficial smile that turned the corners of a curved, mobile mouth showing a flash of even white teeth and faded instantly before it reached his eyes.

'Leave the cleaning today, please. I don't want to be disturbed!'

His voice was as darkly rich as his thatch of black hair. Apparently confident that he'd dismissed her, he strode back into Drummond's office, closing the door firmly behind him.

For ten seconds Tamar stood astounded. As secretary to the group advertisement director she was used to being treated with respect, and even if her appearance did fall beneath her usual standards she wasn't going to be barked at like that. Who the hell did he think he was, anyway? Even if he was a new group head, appointed in her absence, and something now warned her he must be a legitimate member of the staff, he had no right at all in Drummond's office, particularly at this unearthly hour of the morning.

'Right,' she muttered, clenching her teeth aggressively. 'You're going to be disturbed, my friend, whether you like it or not!'

He was sitting in Drummond's chair as she burst into the room, tilting it backwards precariously against the window-frame. His legs were on the desk, ankles crossed. In front of him were piled the contents of her filing-cabinet.

Drawing in her breath with a hiss of displeasure, Tamar observed one of the folders open on his thigh as she rushed into speech.

'Let's get this straight, shall we?' Her stance was belligerent, her small jaw taut with outrage. 'I'm not here to clean the office. My name is Tamar Phillipson and I happen to be Hugh Drummond's secretary.' She saw the dark eyebrows rise slightly, and she had a strong impression that behind the otherwise blank expression on his face, the subject of her displeasure was finding her performance amusing rather than intimidating.

She met his blue-eyed stare with the full authority of her own grey eyes. 'Unless you can give me a satisfactory explanation as to who you are and what you're doing here within the next few seconds, I intend to phone Security!' she challenged coldly.

'Do you, indeed?' The cool response was presumably meant to show he wasn't frightened by her threat. Perhaps it was intended to intimidate her? In fact, all it did was strengthen her resolve.

'Well?' she prompted, her voice edged with exasperation, aware that her obvious duty was to report him, but some inborn caution warning her not to be too precipitate.

The well-formed mouth pursed slightly. 'Tamar Phillipson,' he mused. 'Worked for the company for six years. Seven O levels, three A levels, efficient, conscientious, loyal and adaptable...'

'So you've been prying into the personnel records, too!' she snapped, not attempting to hide her growing hostility.

'Only those that particularly interested me.' There was a studied impertinence in the way he moved his glance down her body. 'There was no mention of dress sense in your file—perhaps advisedly so.'

Tamar's lips tightened angrily at the discourteous comment. She wasn't about to explain the reasons for her casual appearance to this maddening man, whoever he was. Speaking slowly and clearly as an indication that her patience was nearly at an end, she walked closer to the desk, placed her hands on its edge, confident that Hugh Drummond would support her for carrying out what was clearly her duty, and, leaning forward, pierced the intruder with eyes that flashed with temper.

'For the last time...will you please identify yourself?'

The long legs moved with such unexpected speed that, momentarily startled, she sprang away from the desk, retreating a few paces before she realised she'd given the impression of flight and forced herself to hold her ground, not in the least reassured when he stood up and walked over towards her, his lean frame towering over her.

'My name is Dagan Carmichael——' he began, stopping when he saw her jaw relax with shock, before adding grimly, 'You look as if that means something to you.'

Wordlessly Tamar returned his appraisal. Oh, yes, the name certainly did mean something to her! Two years previously INI had been taken over by a Canadian publishing company owned and run by the redoubtable Adrian Conte, whose reputation for ruthlessness in his business life had become legend in the newspaper world. While his sharp intellect masterminded the policy of his world-wide titles, its practical application was carried out by his personal assistant and henchman—Dagan Carmichael.

For the past two years INI had been left in peace, lazy and contented in a false paradise while Conte busied himself with acquisitions in other parts of the globe. Now it seemed their time for reckoning had arrived with a vengeance.

Dagan Carmichael wasn't nicknamed the Dragon Man simply because of his unusual Christian name. His reputation as a fire-breathing, flame-throwing powerhouse of chaos was amply authenticated by his record. He went into Conte's companies, and when he left them they were pared down to the bone of lean efficiency and sharpened to an acme of performance, as if he moulded them in the likeness of his own undoubtedly superb physique, Tamar thought grudgingly.

In the process, it was said, people lost their jobs without thought or compassion. INI had always shown an avuncular interest in its employees. Dagan Carmichael's presence foreshadowed an end to that.

'I read the trade press,' she said eventually, snapping her mouth shut in a disapproving line.

'Then you'll understand the present position very quickly,' he returned smoothly. Did she fancy she saw the brilliant eyes narrow slightly in acknowledgement of her sharp retort? 'When Hugh Drummond returned from the Caribbean yesterday afternoon, he resigned from INI. Adrian Conte has drafted me to take over from him for the time being.'

Hugh resigned, and only yesterday! Impossible to disguise her consternation. Tamar had imagined the man before her must have joined the company in some kind of supervisory capacity while she had been away—but not as a replacement for the existing director. Oh, yes, she was sure she *did* understand the position!

'Do you mean resigned or was relieved of his position?' she asked incautiously, the sheer ruthlessness of what she suspected making her unable to hold her tongue.

'Let's just say he and Adrian had a disagreement over policy and decided to terminate their association.' The smooth answer confirmed her worst fears. Resignation, indeed! Conte or his hatchet-man must have met Hugh at the airport on his return from holiday and, with the swiftness of a cobra striking, relieved him of his directorship. Doubtless a large golden handshake had been given, and Dagan Carmichael had been standing by ready to step into his still warm shoes.

Hugh had been a pleasant man to work for. A little distant and formal—but a good boss. He would find his sudden dismissal humiliating, however much the handshake had glistened, and in his late fifties he might not be able to find re-employment at that level easy.

Aware that the expressions flitting across her face were being watched with intense interest, Tamar took a deep breath to steady her voice.

'Since your appointment is of such recent date, you'll understand I couldn't be expected to know who you were,' she said stiffly in case he was waiting for some kind of apology.

'They don't publish photographs in the trade press?' he mocked her, presumably fully aware that most editors liked to include his handsome profile with their articles concerning his achievements.

'Perhaps they didn't do you justice, or perhaps I hardly anticipated the thrill of coming face to face with you,' she retorted swiftly. She might have added 'at seven-thirty in the morning', but thought better of it.

Her sarcasm didn't go unnoticed or unpunished.

'I can assure you the thrill is mutual.' His glance was deliberately scathing and she felt herself colour beneath the scorn of the sweeping appraisal that lingered on the creased, travel-worn jeans that sat tightly on her slim body. 'All the dailies carried details of my appointment.' The corners of his mouth dimpled unexpectedly. 'All slanted with their own interpretation. I suggest, for the bare, unvarnished facts you read page two of our own publication—that will put you completely in the picture as far as necessary.'

'Of course,' she said sweetly. 'Doubtless you dictated it yourself.'

'Naturally,' he agreed tersely. 'I also read the proof before publication, so its details are entirely accurate. All enquiries during the day are to be referred back to that—and that alone. And now,' he glanced down at the gold watch encircling his hair-darkened, sinewy wrist, 'as I've been here since two o'clock this morning, I'd like two rounds of bacon sandwiches and plenty of coffee. Organise it, will you, please, Miss Phillipson? Then you can bring your book in—we've got a great deal to accomplish today.'

Apparently the interview was ended, for he walked back to the desk, settled his long length in the padded, executive armchair, lifted his legs to rest on the desk and picked up the file he had discarded at her entrance.

Fuming, Tamar stared at him. The time was barely gone seven-thirty. The daytime messenger staff wouldn't have started, and she would have to go down to the works canteen herself to get his food. That didn't bother her, but to expect her to start work immediately afterwards was just too much! If it hadn't been for an accident of fate, she wouldn't even have been in the office at this hour!

'Well?' he snapped, suddenly sensing she was still there and obviously resenting the fact she hadn't run to do his bidding. 'Any problems?'

'I don't officially start work until nine-thirty——' she began heatedly, only to be interrupted.

'Hell! Don't say they've wished a Marxist on me!'

He looked so furious, Tamar felt a wave of warmth lick through her body. He certainly kept his temper on a short leash. All her hackles rose in protest. Not used to being shouted at, she resented his attitude enormously.

'If by that remark you're implying a wilful lack of co-operation, I'd like to remind you that it's not yet eight o'clock in the morning. I've probably had an even more disturbed night than you. I've endured a seemingly endless journey across Europe, undergone the traumatic experience of an emergency landing in the middle of Germany, waited ages to get through Customs and been forced to come directly here because there was no time to get back to my flat and get properly changed as I'd originally planned!' Her voice was beginning to rise uncontrollably, and she fought to steady it. It would be humiliating if he should discount her as a stupid hysteric. 'Then I come in here to discover my office is open and the confidential filing-cabinet to which I have one of the only three keys in the building has been opened and the contents removed!'

Not only that, but a man she had liked and respected had been summarily dismissed! Unbelievably Tamar felt a choking sensation in her throat, as if she were going to burst into tears.

'Then, after all her problems in the wood, Little Red Riding Hood arrives at her nice, comfortable sanctuary only to find it occupied by a dragon!' The deep voice of her tormentor mocked her distress with a cynical humour that shook her.

Really, the man was infuriating, laughing at her. She wasn't surprised he should know his nickname, but she was taken aback that he should refer to it so openly, almost as if he were proud of the havoc that followed in his wake. She gave him a quick glance from lowered lashes, uncertain as to the real state of his temper. All she did know was that the day was rapidly deteriorating and might soon be beyond redemption. Heaven forbid she should be given her cards before her bank balance had recovered from her expensive Greek holiday!

A quick glance at Dagan Carmichael's face showed a derisive smile tugging at the corners of his expressive mouth, as if he were getting pleasure out of her discomfort.

'Better a dragon than a wolf, though—eh, Miss Phillipson?' he queried gently. 'Or are you better equipped to deal with the latter?'

'From what I've read, you're both animals under the same skin!'

As soon as the words were out of her mouth, Tamar regretted them. Her tone had been downright rude and the taunt wasn't worthy of her, neither had it been a sensible accusation to make, however justified. She was a fool to let him nettle her.

Surprisingly, he threw back his head and laughed with what appeared to be genuine appreciation, while she stood there shaking slightly from the shock of his reaction.

'And you didn't read *that* in the trade press!' he retorted, seemingly flattered by what she'd seen as an insult.

No, she'd read it in a weekly magazine featuring the world's most eligible bachelors. Dagan Carmichael— thirty-four, rich, attractive, never long enough in one country to put down roots, but never short of beautiful women to escort to the hot night-spots of the world. Love them and leave them—the epitome of the kind of man she most disliked.

Taking advantage of his sudden good humour, but refusing to pander to his ego, she said firmly, 'Mr Carmichael, I too would like to have some breakfast.

I'd also like some time to read the article you recommended to me.'

'That seems reasonable, Miss Phillipson.' He was matching her coolness, but his eyes were bright with unclouded amusement. 'Am I to expect you to start work sharp at nine-thirty?'

'I'm no clock-watcher,' she returned shortly. 'I'll start as soon as I've had something to eat...and...' She hesitated, feeling the warm blood begin to rise to her cheeks.

'Another condition, Miss Phillipson?'

He was using her surname as a kind of weapon, as if by its continual repetition he placed her in an inferior position.

'Yes,' she told him firmly, making an effort to face him squarely, defying him to make any adverse comment. 'I'd like to make use of your private shower, if I may.'

'Please,' the guarded blankness of expression was almost as bad as if he had made some snide remark, 'consider yourself my guest—Miss Phillipson—any time.'

When Pamela arrived, ten minutes late, and stuck her smiling face round the door, it was to see Tamar elegantly dressed in an oatmeal suit, her high-heeled shoes a perfect match to the dark chocolate satin blouse that showed at her neck. The older girl glanced up as the door opened, her deep honey-coloured hair, freshly washed and blown dry, a shining frame to her face.

'Welcome back, Tammy!' Pamela's round face creased into a grin. 'Sorry I'm late—there's a hold-up on the Tube. Did you have a super holiday?'

'Super,' Tamar told her, smiling. 'You'd better come in and be prepared for a shock.'

'You met a gorgeous Greek god type, and you're engaged to be married!' Pam tended to have a one-track mind.

Tamar shook her head wearily, holding out the newspaper with the paragraph of Dagan Carmichael's appointment circled in red.

'Read this, and all will be explained.'

'Oh, heavens!' Pamela's dark eyes went round with surprise as they assimilated the details.

'Not only has Mr Carmichael superseded Hugh Drummond as group advertisement director of the three titles in question—one daily and two Sundays—but his responsibilities do not end there. He has been given the newly created title of chief executive, and his expanded brief includes keeping a watchful eye on the progress of both circulation and publicity departments. While the editorial departments will continue to enjoy their traditional rights of freedom, it is understood that Mr Carmichael's authority is second only to Adrian Conte's over the entire INI empire.'

Pamela raised her eyes and said, 'Wow!' Then, turning, she pointed a finger at the communicating door. Her voice dropped to a respectful whisper. 'And he's in there now?' she asked.

Grimly Tamar nodded. 'He is.'

'What's he like?' Pamela still appeared stunned by what she had read, and who could blame her?

'Demanding,' Tamar told her drily. 'Autocratic, short-tempered and demanding!'

CHAPTER TWO

AT ONE o'clock Tamar sent Pam off to lunch. Although her junior returned promptly at two, it wasn't until half an hour later that Tamar felt that she herself had reduced the workload sufficiently to take her own break.

Whereas the canteen, open to all but patronised mainly by the printing staff, was large and noisy, with highly subsidised prices, the staff restaurant to which Tamar now made her way was furnished like a commercial concern and boasted waitress service. Prices were subsidised here too, but not to the same degree.

Many of the executive staff and their secretaries tended to take later lunch hours, and it was with a sense of pleasure that Tamar saw Linda Charles seated alone at a table. Linda, secretary to the advertising manager, would prove a valuable source of information on the morning's events as they affected the rest of the department.

'For heaven's sake, Tammy, what's going on?' Linda's reaction to her arrival at the table was sharp and to the point. 'The whole place is in a furore! Do you know five representatives have left already—cleared their desks and gone!'

'So soon?' Tamar's heart plummeted, her worst fears realised as she paused to order an omelette and salad before turning her attention back to her friend. 'I know Carmichael's got a reputation as a butcher, but that must be a record even for him! You mean he just sacked them?'

Linda shrugged. 'According to Mike, he laid down conditions which they found unacceptable—and that meant *out*.'

'What about Mike himself?' Tamar asked anxiously. The advertising manager at thirty was married with two small children. He was a popular and hardworking executive who surely didn't deserve an upheaval of this quality in his life.

'Oh, he's OK,' Linda confirmed with a bright smile. 'He's one hundred per cent behind the Dragon Man. Says it's just what INI need—a good shake-up. I imagine Mike's job is safe enough, provided he performs up to standard, of course.'

'Of course,' Tamar agreed. 'What we've all got to find out now is just how high that standard is going to be.' She accepted her lunch from the waitress with a murmur of thanks.

'What about you, Tam?' Linda asked sympathetically. 'It can't be easy coming back from holiday and finding yourself working for another boss. Will you stay with him?'

It was a question that had crossed Tamar's mind at intervals during the morning. Would she in fact even be given the choice? she had wondered grimly. Her first meeting with Dagan Carmichael had hardly been auspicious.

'I'm thinking about it,' she said guardedly, wishing she had the courage to follow her instincts and tell the Dragon Man exactly what she thought of high-powered executives who came into a company and committed mayhem. 'I don't like his business ethics, but my prospects of finding a similar job in the same industry are very limited, and I'm not over-keen to move into another field.'

'How about going to the other side of the fence?' Linda suggested. 'You could work for an advertising agency, with your expertise.'

'Mmm.' Tamar was non-committal. She had been told often enough that there would always be a job for her at Hathaway Childs, although Neil Hathaway's invitations were hardly altruistic. Knowing she wasn't prepared to have an affair with him, it would hardly be fair to approach Neil for work. He would probably think she'd had a change of heart, not aware that, since what had happened with Martin, she had resolved never to get involved with anyone working for the same company. Besides, if Neil used his influence as the managing director's son to find her a position, the rest of the agency staff would probably resent her—and she wouldn't blame them for that.

'I'll have to go.' Linda finished her coffee. 'I've been co-opted into helping the secretaries in the reps' room. Do you know,' she leaned over the table confidentially, 'your Dagan's made all the reps postpone every appointment they've made unless it can be justified before him as urgent, until all their agency reports are up to date. You can't imagine the backlog that exists!' She grinned wickedly. 'Honestly, the reps' room looks like a sixth-form evening prep, eyes down, heads bent over desks. They're not even being allowed to dictate because they're so behindhand. Carmichael says they've got to write each report out by hand and then get the girls to type them. Even then, it's too much for Mandy and Karen alone, so I'm doing my stint too.' She stood up, 'It occurs to me that the local pub takings are going to be down this week and a lot of golf games aren't going to get played. Mike might just be right at that, you know,' she added thoughtfully. 'Perhaps INI did need your Dagan, after all!'

Her Dagan, indeed! INI might have needed him, Tamar thought mutinously, watching Linda's departing back, but *she* certainly didn't! As far as she was concerned, he was an alien intruder into what had previously been a pleasant working ambience. In place of the gentlemanly Hugh Drummond, INI was faced with a tough and brash operator, and she only hoped her colleagues were able to handle him better than she had done to date.

So far the only thing in his favour had been the ungrudging permission she had received to use his private shower. It was probably the fastest shower she'd ever taken in her life. Even with the door firmly bolted, standing there naked she'd been very conscious that she was only a few yards away from his overbearing masculine presence. It had been an unnerving experience, and she could only explain her reactions by assuming they were an aftermath of her ordeal in the plane.

Finishing the coffee which had come with her meal, she rose to her feet. She had only taken a half-hour break, but a sense of duty drove her back to the office. The morning had been devoted to ensuring that everyone in the department was aware of the new management structure, and the majority had been given the opportunity of meeting their new chief executive face to face.

The next step was consolidation with the advertising agencies, necessitating a mixture of personal letters and phone calls. That was apart from answering all the incoming calls. Pamela was a stalwart assistant, but she did tend to panic—and in these circumstances well she might.

Contrary to her fears, all was quiet when Tamar re-entered the office.

'He's still in there,' Pam told her in hushed tones. 'I know because he's had the phone switched through and the extension light's still on.'

'You haven't actually met him yet?' asked Tamar, interested in her young assistant's reaction to such a powerful force.

'No. He's been using the other exit from his office, directly into the executive corridor. He hasn't been in here at all.'

Tamar nodded, a glow of satisfaction spreading through her. It seemed the Dragon Man was satisfied with what they had achieved that morning, anyway.

It was past four o'clock when Pamela walked through into Tamar's room with a pile of addressed envelopes and laid them on her desk. 'I've been thinking, Tam...' she nodded at the phone where the engaged light continued to show '...he hasn't even been out to lunch. Do you think we should ask him if he wants anything to eat?'

'Why?' Tamar's shapely eyebrows rose interrogatively. 'I can assure you Dagan Carmichael's quite capable of asking for what he wants. If the man's hungry, you can be sure he's going to let us know.' She pressed the relevant key of her electronic typewriter, watching the paper shoot up to its correct position. 'In my opinion, the position of secretary is too often confused with that of nursemaid or mother, and I can assure you, Pam, that my feelings for Mr Carmichael are not in the least maternal!'

'And I can assure *you*, Miss Phillipson, that I would be extremely disappointed if they were!'

Pamela gasped as Tamar felt the hot tide of embarrassment flood her cheeks with colour.

Unheard by either girl, Dagan Carmichael had emerged from his den to stand in the communicating doorway, one hand resting over his head on the lintel, the other pressed into the small of his back, as if he was stretching his tired muscles. He looked big and tough and awe-inspiring.

Tamar clenched her jaw. She wouldn't apologise. She just wouldn't. Her remark had been ill-timed and she regretted he'd overheard it, but in itself it was nothing but the truth. Fortunately, after his first remark he ignored her, his deep blue eyes fastening on Pamela, who stared at him as if he were an apparition.

'You must be Pamela,' he said easily, his mouth moving into a beguiling smile as she nodded. 'I think you must be one of the very last members of staff I've still to see today, but then I always try to leave the best till last.'

Pamela wriggled self-consciously, unable to hide her pleasure. Like a silly little poodle that's just been patted, Tamar thought uncharitably. Pamela was old enough at seventeen to recognise insincerity when she saw it. How could she fall for such a hackneyed line? But Dagan had more to come.

'You've been with us for nearly a year now, I believe?'

'Yes, Mr Carmichael,' Pamela found her voice at last.

'And very good reports I've read about you.' The deep voice was warm. 'From the way you've pulled your weight today I can see they're justified. As soon as things have settled on an even keel, we'll have to see about getting you an increase.'

'Oh!' Again he had made Pamela speechless. She stood there, her mouth slightly open, as if she were seeing an incarnation of Bob Geldof and the Messiah all in one.

How could she fall for such applied charm? Tamar wondered in despair. Surely such avid worship would irritate this sophisticated tyrant? But no. If anything, his expression had softened even further, and now she could see and be startled by the sweep of his dark eyelashes as he narrowed his eyes speculatively.

'I wonder if you could possibly rustle me up something to eat, Pamela?'

Was it coincidence, or had he heard all their conversation? Tamar kept her eyes fastened on the paper in her typewriter.

'Yes, of course,' Pam breathed. 'In fact, I was just saying...' She broke off rapidly as a sharp stiletto glare directed from her colleague pierced through her euphoria. 'That is,' she gulped, 'what would you like? I can get you a cooked meal from the works canteen. It's really very good—and cheap too,' she added, seemingly unaware of the incongruity of the information to someone who regularly dined at international Hiltons. 'They do a splendid steak pie and chips, or fish and chips, or...'

'I see you have all the instincts of a real woman,' Dagan murmured, causing Pam's colour to ebb and flow with surprising rapidity. 'But no, just sandwiches, please. Ham, beef...' He shrugged. 'I'll leave the choice to you—and coffee, of course!'

With a disarming show of perfect white teeth, he prised himself away from the door-frame and backed into his office without another glance in Tamar's direction.

It was only after Pamela had fulfilled her task and taken the snack into the inner sanctum that the younger girl returned to confront her colleague.

'Oh, Tammy, why didn't you tell me? He's beautiful!'

'That's strictly a matter of personal opinion.'

'Oh, come on! With that face and that physique he could make the centrefold of *Playgirl* any day.'

'I wouldn't know.' Aware that she sounded stiff and priggish, Tamar allowed her face to relax into a rueful smile. 'Well, maybe,' she admitted. 'He does have a kind of compelling magnetism, but then I imagine most dragons do—but I wouldn't care to stroke one.'

'I'd stroke Dagan Carmichael any time he asked me to,' Pamela said dreamily. 'And allow him the same privilege in return!' She gave an explicit little shiver that put Tamar's teeth on edge.

'I think it's about time you finished the rest of those envelopes, or you're going to find out that your pet dragon can roar—and maybe even bite!' It wasn't often she spoke sharply to Pamela, but her nerves were screaming and there was still so much she wanted to finish before she went home. As the younger girl went back to her own office, Tamar bent her head over the work in front of her and tried to concentrate.

It was six-thirty when her task was finished, an hour after Pamela had made her own departure. Pushing the door of Dagan's office open, after a brief tap, Tamar entered, the last of the urgent letters for signature in her hands. He wasn't at his desk, but the bathroom door was open and she could hear running water. Well, that was fine. She would just leave the letters on his desk and go.

She was half-way back to her own office when he emerged from the bathroom to stand in front of her, blocking her path.

'Are you off home now, Miss Phillipson, or can you spare me a few moments?'

He was stripped to the waist, a towel slung round his neck, his black hair showing signs of dampness. The five-o'clock shadow that had darkened his strong jaw had vanished. His facial skin was taut and gleaming with health, lightly tanned and spicily scented. She would have been blind not to notice the smoothly corrugated structure of his chest, the sleekly cushioned muscles of his arms as they interleaved with the precision of dove-tail joints; and she wasn't blind, although she began to doubt the soundness of her other senses. Surely this drumming in her ears was unusual. And her legs didn't normally feel as weak as this, did they?

Dagan Carmichael seemed totally unaware that he was under-dressed for an office, but there was nothing intrinsically improper in his appearance, she lectured herself sternly. She should be able to take it in her stride. Desperately she tried to find something to say, but all she could think of was Pamela's remark about the centre-fold. If Pam could only see him now—like this!

'Something amuses you, Miss Phillipson?' he asked gently, his eyes innocently enquiring.

'You must excuse me,' she returned quickly, killing the smile that had unwittingly curved her full lips. 'The thought of actually going home and getting some sleep made me slightly hysterical. Yes, that was my intention.' She met his eyes boldly. 'I've just a few more papers to tidy away, but if it's important I'm quite willing to spare you a few moments.'

He gave her a straight look from those piercing blue eyes before nodding abruptly. 'Finish your tidying, then, and come back.'

He was still in the bathroom when she returned, his deep voice reaching out to her. 'I don't suppose among your many talents you can tie a bow-tie, can you, Miss Phillipson?'

Tamar suppressed a smile. A year ago it would have been a mystery to her. She had Neil Hathaway to thank for her present level of expertise.

'Of course, Mr Carmichael,' she replied sweetly, feeling extraordinarily pleased with herself.

'Then I shall be forever in your debt!'

As he emerged from the bathroom, it was all she could do not to gasp. In a lounge suit he'd been arresting, stripped to the waist he'd been compelling, in black evening trousers and white frilled shirt he was devastating! Between lean, tanned fingers hung the evidence of his failure.

Wordlessly, Tamar took the strip of black silk, reaching to place it round his neck, aware that his proximity was doing strange, painful things to her. What other situation was there that would allow two people of the opposite sex to stand so close to each other without amorous intentions? she wondered. Unaccountably her fingers trembled.

'I know the principle of the darned thing,' Dagan was muttering crossly. 'But when you try and do it with a mirror, everything's reversed!' He made it sound as if he had discovered some new scientific fact, as Tamar suppressed a wild desire to giggle.

'What do you usually do?' she asked instead. 'Wear a made-up one?'

'Hardly!' He sounded outraged, shaking his head in violent negation, causing her to lose hold of one of the ends.

'Oh!' Her own exasperation rose to meet his own. If this was all he had wanted from her, she wished she'd gone home earlier. 'Please keep still.'

'Sorry,' he said meekly. 'No, I generally find my lady friends are very skilled in the art of tie-tying. Unfortunately this evening is purely stag—the Board of INI.'

Trust him to have his lady friends organised to administer to his needs! This time Tamar didn't try to stop her smile. 'There!' Triumphantly she stepped away from him, glad to escape from the close magnetic pull he seemed to exercise on her. 'That looks perfect.'

'Thanks.' He didn't even trouble to touch it, striding immediately towards the built-in cocktail cabinet that graced one side of his large office. 'Now, what would you like to drink? You probably know what's in here better than I do.' He peered inside at the assortment of bottles and mixers.

For a moment Tamar hesitated. She drank very little on normal occasions, but then this was hardly normal. 'Scotch and dry ginger, please,' she said, obeying his gesture and seating herself on the luxurious cream leather couch against the wall, watching as he poured out two similar drinks. Instead of returning to his own desk as she had expected, he surprised her by sitting down beside her, splaying his long legs and placing his free arm along the back of the couch. Instinctively she tensed.

'Well, Miss Phillipson.' He motioned her to clink glasses before lifting his to take a long swallow, then, turning sideways, he gave her the full battery of his startling eyes. 'Are you going to work with me—or not?'

It was the question she had been posing to herself without settling on a solution: only she hadn't expected to be faced with making a decision so soon. An odd premonition warned her that, if the strange physical reactions Dagan Carmichael's presence seemed to be causing her that evening were going to be the norm, they would both be better off if she left.

'That depends,' she temporised, deciding to throw the ball back into his court. 'Do you want me to stay?'

'Yes—on certain conditions.' He sounded strangely grim.

'You want to change my job specification?' she hazarded. 'Hours, duties...?'

'Nothing like that.' He hesitated. 'You may have heard that several members of staff left today.' Then, as she nodded, 'I have to say the same thing to you as I said to them, and I have to ask you to make an honest decision. I've been given a difficult and challenging task here. To fulfil it I must have total loyalty not only to myself while I stay here, but wholeheartedly to the company. If you resent my being put in this position, if you feel Hugh Drummond was badly treated, if you harbour any grudge against the present management and are not prepared to give them your total, unstinting support—then there's no room for you here at INI.' His voice softened, became more informal. 'In a nutshell, you're either with me—or against me. And if it's the latter, then there's no way we can work together.'

Tamar sucked in her breath. She *did* resent the cavalier way her previous boss had been treated, but surely her sense of grievance on his behalf wouldn't affect her own loyalty to INI?

'That's the ultimatum you gave to the other staff?' She was playing for time, uncertainty twisting inside her.

Dagan nodded. 'That's it. Some had personal loyalties to Drummond that they couldn't or wouldn't transfer. They decided to leave and I respect them for that decision. The majority stayed.' A brief smile flitted across his lips. 'Not all for the right reasons. Some did support me wholeheartedly, others were hesitant but too unsure of their ability to throw themselves on to the job market, a few may even have stayed for the sole purpose of giving me a bad time and hoping to see me fail.'

Amazed at his perspicacity, Tamar asked wonderingly, 'And you can identify these different types?'

'In time I will, never doubt it...in time.' His hand dropped from the couch to rest impersonally on her shoulder, but beneath its warmth she felt her skin quiver and prayed he hadn't felt it too. 'In particular I would like *you* to stay on. Your experience in the job is going to be invaluable to me. But only if I have your total loyalty.' He gave her a sudden charming grin that made her catch her breath. 'I tend to work very closely with my secretaries, have no secrets from them. That makes me very vulnerable and I can't afford to take chances.'

Anyone less vulnerable than Dagan Carmichael was hard to imagine. But at least in his favour he hadn't sacked the people who had left, just allowed them to make their own gesture of defiance before he ventured the ship of INI out into the stormy seas that awaited her. That was common sense, not cruelty. Had she misjudged him? Looking into his bland, enquiring face, she decided she hadn't, but she did feel the first seeds of admiration beginning to root in her mind. The newspaper industry had been turned inside-out by recent technical advances, production was cheaper but there were more papers being born which needed the nourishment of advertising revenue to grow to a healthy maturity, and there was only a limited amount of that nourishment to be shared among the growing brood. INI would have to fight hard for their share, which was why Adrian Conte had replaced his top man with a hard-bitten mercenary.

A thrill of expectation tingled through Tamar's tired limbs. To work with Dagan Carmichael in the battle ahead would be exciting and challenging. There was no prerequisite that she should have to like him!

As if from a great distance, she heard herself say politely, 'I see no difficulty in accepting those conditions, Mr Carmichael.'

'Good!' He drained the rest of the liquid from his glass. 'How do you prefer to be called—Tamar or Tammy?'

Confused, she stammered, 'It doesn't matter, I—I answer to either.'

'Then I'll play it by mood.' He smiled a wicked twist of his firm mouth. 'Tammy when we're friends—Tamar when I'm furious with you.'

She managed a small smile in reply, not particularly happy about the forecast that he might be furious with her at some future date—it suggested too volatile a relationship for her liking, but he was continuing to speak, laying down the foundations for their future business association. 'I'm not a particularly formal person, Tammy. I like to think my office door is always open and I'm there for anyone with a problem, and I expect to be called by my Christian name by senior staff.'

'Yes, Mr Carmichael,' Tammy said docilely, earning herself a sharp glance, which she pretended not to have seen.

'Where exactly do you live, Miss Phillipson?' Dagan accented her surname with heavy irony.

She named the south London suburb where her flat was located.

'Then finish your drink and I'll drive you home.'

'Oh, no!' Truly horrified, she jumped to her feet. 'That's quite unnecessary. I mean to get the Tube.'

'My dear Tammy, it's entirely necessary,' he responded impatiently. 'Not only have you had a traumatic journey back to this country, you've worked unremittingly with the shortest of breaks, and I've kept you well past normal office hours. You also have a heavy suitcase to transport and you look exhausted.' He raised a hand to still further protests. 'If you're going to work happily with me, you're going to have to learn to accept my decisions without question, but for this once I shall point out that if I so wished I could get a chauffeur from the pool to drive you home. As it is, I've plenty of time before this dinner with the board starts, and I find driving relaxing. So stop arguing and get your coat on!'

Tamar had no option but to obey. And he was right— it had been an exhausting and disquieting day.

He drove well and she relaxed beside him, feeling no need for conversation. Parking outside her flat, he carried her suitcase up to the front door. Thanking him, she was grateful he had another engagement, so there was no need to ask him out of politeness if he would like to come inside for a few minutes.

'Do you want me in early tomorrow?' It was the least she could offer.

He shook his head. 'No, the usual time will do.' He bent his head towards her, his face warmly attractive. 'If I do ever want anything more from you than your contract covers, be sure I'll let you know, Tammy.'

For one absurd heart-stopping moment she thought he was going to kiss her, and almost shut her eyes in anticipation. Then he was gone, striding lean and dynamic down the path.

Win your secretary over and she'll smooth your path, she thought cynically as she carried her case up the stairs. It had been a good public relations exercise accomplished by Dagan, and she admired him for the effort he had made. But admiring was one thing, liking and respecting something else. She was no Pamela to be fooled by his easy, insincere charm. Dagan Carmichael had come to INI with a fearful reputation. It would take a great deal to persuade Tamar that he didn't merit every bit of it.

CHAPTER THREE

WITH practised fingers Tamar flicked through Dagan's personal diary, glimpsing the names she'd become familiar with over the past three months—Geraldine, Sara and Pauline. She thought, not for the first time, that he obviously believed in safety in numbers, as their names were dispersed evenly throughout the book, absently wondering which one tied the best bow-tie.

She had no idea where he'd met them, and it was, of course, none of her business. Dagan was renowned for playing as hard as he worked, but it seemed he was wise enough to insist that his playmates never troubled him at the office, and obviously they all valued his 'friendship' sufficiently to obey him. Idly she wondered which one of the three would be chosen to accompany him to the annual staff Christmas dinner-dance which was shortly to be held at a large London hotel.

It hardly seemed possible that Christmas should be looming on the horizon so soon, but then for the past weeks she had been kept so busy, time had simply flown by. Already Dagan Carmichael's success was beginning to be reflected in the slow but steady increase of advertising revenue and the more efficient, dynamic approach of the advertisement staff. To do him justice, his reputation as a slave-driver wasn't entirely merited, Tamar admitted to herself. Unless one expected a slave-driver to work harder than the men he directed. For work Dagan certainly did, and it was noticeable there was little room in his day for the long so-called business lunches that had been a main feature of Hugh Drummond's life, although he did occasionally fit in the rare personal appointment.

As time progressed she had found herself enjoying working with him. He wasn't always easy to please, but she was learning to ride his bouts of impatience. As he had foretold, she was fully in his confidence, keeping both his business and personal diaries and being *au fait* with all the problems of his busy life.

Yet she never took him for granted. Never felt totally at ease in his company. Dagan Carmichael was too powerful for her to be complacent. Mentally and physically strong, he appeared to have little patience for anyone who fell below his own stringent standards. Alone, she admitted, he would have been formidable, but with the added power of Adrian Conte's authority channelled through him, at times he quivered like an overheated dynamo. Exhilarating—yes! Comfortable— never. Yet when he walked into the office Tamar's day took on an added dimension, something that had never happened with Hugh Drummond.

Not wanting to question her reactions too closely, Tamar snapped the diary closed, opening the business one instead to check through the present day's appointments, noting that Dagan would be arriving later because of a working breakfast at the Savoy with the chairman of an important American chemical company. That would give her another half-hour to finish sorting the post and making the phone calls he'd left for her.

She'd just finished when her own phone rang.

'Tammy?' Neil Hathaway's voice sounded over the wire. 'Well, it's great to hear you answer your own phone for a change. I was beginning to think the Dragon Man had locked you away somewhere *incommunicado*!'

'I'm sorry, Neil,' she smiled wryly. 'The last few months have been really hectic. I've hardly had a chance to breathe, let alone socialise.'

'So I've noticed,' he commented ruefully. 'You've already turned me down on the last half-dozen occasions I've asked you out.'

'I'm sure you found a replacement for me,' she answered lightly. 'I know you've never short of girlfriends, Neil. In fact, I thought you'd probably given me up as a bad job.'

'Don't you believe it! I'm like most of my kind—the unavailable holds a stronger attraction for me than the easily obtainable!'

Tamar laughed. 'I'm not exactly unavailable, Neil, just difficult to pin down in the present climate.'

'Well, I'm about to try and pin you down right now, Tammy, and I won't take no for an answer. I want to be your partner to the annual shindig INI lay on at Christmas. Is that possible—or has the boss reserved that favour for himself as well?'

'Hardly.' She heard the door in the outer office close. 'Look, Neil, Pam's just come back with some urgent statistics from publicity, and I have to go. I'd love you to be my escort. Can you pick me up about six? That should give us plenty of time.'

'I'd be delighted,' His voice oozed self-satisfaction. 'You and I have a lot of catching up to do.'

'I'll look forward to it. Bye, Neil.' She was still smiling as she replaced the receiver and turned to come face to face with Dagan.

In return for her bright, 'Good morning,' she received an indistinct grunt.

'When you've finished making your private phone calls I'd like to see you in my office.' He walked past her, his face stern.

How typical of Dagan, Tamar thought angrily, to walk up the eight flights of stairs that meant he had to enter his suite through her office rather than take the executive lift which carried him directly to his own door.

She knew he had walked because of the air of virtue that cloaked him—the holier-than-thou complacency of the early-morning jogger. She just lived for the day when he would come in out of breath! Surely, the way he burned the candle at both ends, that wouldn't be far off? But it clearly wasn't today. He merely glowed with rude health and vigour. Still, something had obviously upset him, and she was soon to find out what.

Smoothing down her scarlet sweater dress and adjusting the patent leather belt that cinched her narrow waist, she picked up her notebook and walked sedately into the inner sanctum. Pretending not to recognise his displeasure, she turned a sweetly smiling face towards his heavy frown, awaiting his attention.

'I've just met Terry Lester in the foyer and learned that we're about to lose our share of the Creta Cosmetics budget.' He came straight to the point as anger tightened the lines round his mouth. 'I'm calling an emergency meeting of advertisement managerial staff for twelve-thirty today in the directors' dining-room. See that lunch is laid on and everyone concerned notified without delay, and mark it "top priority". Cancel my existing lunch date.' Head bent over her book, Tammy quickly made the relevant notes. That would be Pauline. Perhaps she would get the dinner-dance as compensation—lucky Pauline! 'And I'd like you to pick up a few odds and ends of shopping for me in your lunch break.' He thrust a folded sheet of paper at her, which she accepted with a sigh.

It wouldn't be the first time she had traipsed around the shops on Dagan Carmichael's behalf. Earlier attempts to pass the chore on to Pamela had met with his disapproval. 'My dear Tammy,' he'd said coolly, 'if I'd wanted Pamela to do my shopping, I'd have asked her. It's your expertise and experience I want—not that of a seventeen-year-old just out of school!'

'Yes, Dagan,' she said now, resignedly, noting that he hadn't said 'please'—a sure sign that he was out of sorts. 'Is that all?'

He shot her a sharp look from ultramarine eyes that glinted with impatience and a touch of temper. 'For the time being, and please bear in mind that I prefer you to organise your love-life in your own time—not mine!'

Before she could draw in a breath or do more than let him see the angry flash of fire in her grey eyes, he had picked up his phone and started dialling.

Keeping her temper under control with an effort, Tamar turned on her heel and left. To lose out on the million-pound budget for Creta was a calamity, but it was no reason for Dagan to take out his fury on her. It wasn't as if she used the phone a lot for her own affairs. Now, if it had been Pamela...

Her thoughts were interrupted by the angry buzzing of the intercom, and Dagan demanding why the expenses claims weren't on his desk for checking. When she weeded out the file from among a wad of computer print-out, he muttered something about part of her duties being to see his desk was kept tidy. Seeing he had given her explicit instructions never to interfere with papers spread over his desk, and before his arrival that morning everything had been in pristine order anyway, she forced herself to ignore his censure.

For the rest of the morning she kept out of his way, using tact and discretion to divert the calls and problems she knew he wouldn't want to be bothered with, and only transferring to him the really urgent decision-making work.

It wasn't until gone twelve that she remembered his shopping list and, relaxing to enjoy her first coffee of the day, opened it out to see what she was expected to find this time.

Dagan, she knew, was renting a bungalow deep in the Surrey countryside. His housekeeper supplied most things, but Dagan had still found it necessary to ask her, Tamar, to pick up what he called 'odds and ends'. In the past these had ranged from presents for his girl-friends to shaving-sticks, batteries and lighter fuel, and on one occasion a three-pound hammer.

Now what would he want? Her eyes travelled down the list—a swan-necked desk-lamp, black silk evening socks, a five-pound box of special hand-made chocolates and—she did a double-take—two pairs of underpants? He actually expected her to go out and buy his underwear now!

She had already made the comparison between a secretary and a wife, but this was taking things too far! She was sitting there stunned when the door between their offices opened and Dagan exploded into the room, shrugging broad shoulders into the jacket of his lounge suit. 'Don't be late back from lunch, will you? This is a working lunch I'm chairing, and I shall want to write up notes just as soon as I return,' he instructed tersely.

'Wait!' Tamar almost shrieked the word, because his rate of progress had nearly taken him out into Pamela's office.

'Well?' He stared back at her, eyebrows a tight band of intolerance, jaw taut with irritation, sensuous mouth pressed into a firm line to indicate that it had better be for something important that she had stopped him in full flight. Beneath his uncompromising glare she started to flounder, to her acute annoyance.

'I—I mean, you want this shopping.' She tapped the list. 'I'll have to go to Regent Street for the chocolates.'

Dagan sighed heavily. 'Then get a cab—is that it?'

'No!' Again her voice had been over-loud, and he made a point of wincing so she should be made aware of it. 'No,' she repeated, controlling her voice into a softer tone. 'The other things you want—socks, for example—I don't know what size.'

'For a size ten shoe. Is that all?' His tone warned her it had better be, but if he couldn't trust his housekeeper or girlfriends to buy his underclothes and couldn't spare the time to do his own intimate shopping, then the least he could do was give her precise details of his requirements.

'Underpants,' she said crisply. 'For yourself, you mean?' Despite her good intentions, she felt a slow wash of colour begin to stain her cheeks.

'No,' he barked sarcastically, 'for the chairman of the board as a Christmas present! For pity's sake, Tammy, who do you think they're for?'

Bravely she ignored his exasperation. 'Well, what kind, then?'

She was damned if she was going to ask him what size! Neither would she dare to let her eyes drift down to that part of the anatomy they would clothe. Behind his impatience she could sense a growing amusement which infuriated her.

'My dear Tammy...' He'd walked softly back to her desk, and, eyes cast down on the list, she hadn't seen his movement until his hands flattened on the surface in front of her and his face appeared inches before her own. Mesmerised as much by the silk flare of jet lashes that bordered the inky blue eyes as by the glinting appraisal to which she was being subjected, Tamar felt the steady pattern of her heartbeat increase to a roll of thunder, as he continued implacably, 'I'm faced with the prospect of losing half a million pounds of advertising revenue, for no better reason than that the advertisement rep of our main competitors happens to be sleeping with the accounts director of the advertising agency responsible for making the appropriation recommendations to the client. In the next forty-eight hours I have to devise a scheme to stop that happening, and all you can do is ask me what kind of underpants I wear!'

Tamar bridled defensively. He was being desperately unfair and, what was more, he was enjoying himself at her expense. Still the deeply probing eyes surveyed her, and now she saw a muscle twitch at the corners of his mobile mouth.

'I don't give a damn what you get,' he bit out softly. 'Since I don't intend appearing in public wearing them without a suitable covering! My housekeeper in Canada did my packing in rather a rush.' A pause and then, 'Use your imagination, or get whatever your own boyfriend wears. Yes,' he nodded with every sign of satisfaction, 'that's it. Get something *you* find attractive, Tammy.' He straightened his back, taking fast, economical strides away from her. 'And don't forget what I said about not being late back.'

Half an hour later she was still furious with him. The loss of the Creta account was calamitous news, but none of her doing, and Terry Lester who handled the agency was one of the best advertisement reps in the business, but if Dagan's allegations were true Terry was hardly in possession of the right attributes to alter the decision. Little wonder Dagan was incensed and was taking out his pique on her simply because she was a woman, as if she were the one having the affair that could re-route half a million!

She hadn't got a cab, knowing that the Tube, though more crowded, would get her up to the West End quicker because of the density of the lunchtime traffic. Well, she had got his lamp, the chocolates and the silk socks. Now she could turn her mind to the *pièce de résistance*. Use your imagination, Dagan had said, and that was exactly what she intended doing. Turning into Oxford Street, she saw just what she wanted—there on a barrow at the side of the road was the largest, brightest selection of men's underclothing she had ever seen in her life.

Forcing her way into the middle of a throng of giggling girls, she viewed the spread with growing delight. So Dagan had left it to her, had he? This wasn't going to take long. Carefully she selected a pair of black nylon briefs with the words 'Get Lost' emblazoned in white silk thread, back and front, and a white pair even briefer which delightfully featured the Canadian maple leaf emblem in bright scarlet, very strategically placed.

'Big lad, is he?' the barrowboy asked her, scribbling out a receipt at her request. 'Shouldn't have any trouble with these. Medium large they are, easily stretching for comfort.' He gave her an evil wink as he handed the change over.

Yes, Dagan was a big lad—and it was about time he started behaving with a suitable maturity when he wanted favours. Tamar wasn't his slave to do his bidding without demur. Hopefully that was the message he would get on opening his purchases.

Returning to the office, she left the goods neatly stacked on the small table in his office, drawing his attention to them before she finally left for the evening. He nodded absently, deeply engrossed in a report, pausing only to wish her goodnight before continuing with his labours.

The following morning she waited for Dagan's reaction, disappointed when he made no reference to her shopping. Either he'd decided to ignore her gesture or he simply hadn't opened his parcels yet, she decided, as she tidied her desk ready to leave.

Today, Friday, had been the last day at work before the Christmas break. The dinner-dance was on Saturday, and she would be catching the train early Sunday morning to travel down to Bournemouth to share the celebrations with her mother, her married sister and the latter's family. After the hectic weeks she had just lived through, the thought of being able to sit back and relax was a welcoming one. To do Dagan credit, he'd made no objection to her having the Christmas Eve Monday off, and even suggested that she should take her time about putting in an appearance on the Thursday.

In fact, the only dull spot on the horizon was the continuing drama of Creta Cosmetics. It was clear that the problem which had been gnawing at everyone's ingenuity during the day would still be with them after the Christmas break. She supposed that kind of disaster was what Dagan was paid a staggering salary to cope with.

She could even find it in her heart to feel sorry for him at that moment.

'You are coming to the do tomorrow, aren't you, Tammy?' asked Pamela, on the point of leaving.

'Wild horses wouldn't stop me!' Smilingly she confirmed it. 'Neil's taking me.'

'I can't wait to see who *he* brings with him.' Pamela gestured confidentially at Dagan's office, sighing dramatically. 'I bet she's absolutely ravishing.'

'I'm sure she is,' Tamar agreed drily. 'Let's just hope she's got a good sense of humour too!'

Refusing to amplify her statement further, she picked up her handbag and made for the exit. 'Come on, Pam. It's the first time since I started working for Dagan Carmichael that I've had the opportunity of leaving on time—and I mean to make the most of it!'

Just over twenty-four hours later, Neil Hathaway, looking superb with his light hair elegantly styled to show off his classic profile, was bringing Tamar a glass of dry sherry from a passing waiter's tray at the pre-dinner reception.

'Just introduced myself to your boss,' he told her easily. 'Told him we'd be getting in touch with him in the New Year to discuss a marketing proposition for Dakitsu electronics.'

'That must have pleased him.' Tamar sipped her drink appreciatively. Naturally she hadn't discussed the Creta catastrophe with her companion, but the advertising world must have heard rumours of INI's impending bad luck.

'Certainly brought a smile to his face,' Neil agreed nonchalantly. 'Seems he's come here alone tonight—no beautiful *femme fatale* on his arm. I guess he intends to spread his favours around among the female staff.'

'Really?' Should she be surprised? Dagan had never allowed any of his girlfriends access to the office. It seemed they fulfilled a need in his personal life but one he had no intention of allowing to overflow into his public business appearances. To introduce one to his fellow directors, to have her gawped at by his staff, would give the girl a false sense of importance about her place in his life, no doubt.

From what Tamar had read about Dagan Carmichael, he would only be looking for one thing from a female companion—and that wouldn't be friendship, companionship or even love.

Thoughtfully she let her gaze wander over the crowd. All the clerical departments of INI were represented, and the vast reception hall was swarming with elegantly dressed men and beautifully gowned women. She couldn't see Dagan, but her eye did alight on Pamela, who was looking a little bemused. A young man wearing his evening dress with rather a self-conscious air stood at her side.

Moving through the crowd, Neil in her wake, Tammy drew alongside her junior and introduced her escort.

'This is Simon,' Pamela reciprocated. 'He's a friend of my brother. Say,' her voice was low, 'this is a bit awe-inspiring, isn't it, Tam?' Her face grew wide-eyed with admiration. 'You look absolutely stunning!'

'Thank you.' Tamar accepted the compliment gracefully. She hadn't meant to buy anything new for the function. Opportunities for wearing formal dress were few and far between in her calendar, and she'd fully intended to wear what she had bought for last year's Christmas dinner. That morning, for a reason she didn't understand, she'd changed her mind, fighting her way through the pre-Christmas crowds at her local shopping centre to her favourite boutique.

Even at that late date the choice had been good, and she found herself faced with a heady selection of glittering garments. The fashion pundits had gone for glamour in a big way: sequins, lamé, gold-encrusted velvets, fishtail nets. Nothing as discreet as the dark blue lace she'd originally planned to wear. For a moment she'd been taken aback at the lack of anything remotely discreet, then her spirit of adventure had triumphed. If this was what was fashionable, then to turn her back on it would date her as much as wearing her skirts mid-calf when everyone else was showing their knees!

She had avoided the extremes, however, selecting a vivid scarlet crêpe cocktail dress, the top sleeveless and lightly boned to flatter her cleavage, with bootlace-thin diamanté straps crossing her shoulders to join the back which skimmed the edge of her shoulderblades. The skirt was straight, but ruched fetchingly from waist to hem, touching her knees to leave her shapely calves encased in twelve-denier nylon to display themselves to advantage in scarlet high-heeled sandals.

She had chosen not to wear anything round her neck, modestly aware that her shoulders and breasts were firmly enough fleshed to stay unadorned. Instead she had contented herself by arranging her hair on top of her head, securing it with a clasp which matched the dangling diamanté earrings she'd fixed to her small ears.

Neil's eyes had lit up most satisfactorily when he had come to pick her up, and Pamela's admiration was gratifying and obviously genuine.

'You look pretty stunning yourself,' she returned generously, noting how well the amber taffeta of her dress set off Pamela's dark eyes and hair. 'There's no need to be nervous. I've just looked at the table plans. You and I are on the same table with Mike Redway, Linda and John Cavendish and their respective partners.'

'That's great!' A look of relief passed across the younger girl's face. 'I was afraid I wouldn't be near anyone I knew.'

Tamar gave her a friendly hug. 'Don't worry, my love. Take my word for it. It's a super do—very informal—everyone has a whale of a time, you'll see.'

Two hours later her prophecy was fulfilled.

'Shall we join the throng?' Neil's arms encircled her shoulders immediately the dessert plates had been cleared and the band began to play. Unlike some affairs she had attended, where it took people a long time to venture on to the floor, here at the first note, the area in the centre of the room became crowded.

There was something volatile and exciting about most newspaper people, Tammy thought wryly, as she accepted Neil's invitation. A creativity, allied to the ability to communicate, which gave them a *joie de vivre* that made for informality.

Her eyes stole to the directors' table, inevitably resting on Dagan, wondering if he would sit for the rest of the evening, talking to his colleagues, or whether, as Neil had surmised he would venture on to the floor. Her query was almost immediately answered as he rose to his feet to lead the wife of the circulation manager towards the crowded dancing area.

As the evening progressed, two things became increasingly clear. The first was that Dagan was a good mover on the dance-floor, coping with the varied assortment of rhythms supplied by the three different bands engaged. He performed calypso, twist, waltz, reggae and Latin-American adequately, if not brilliantly. Perhaps walking up eight flights of stairs had been his way of training for this marathon exhibition, she thought none too kindly, and wondered why she should feel so resentful because he was enjoying himself so much.

The second thing was that he obviously intended to spread his intentions equally among the wives of his immediate staff and the girls who worked throughout his department. With a bit of luck, Tamar thought waspishly, he would be exhausted by the time he got round to *her* table. Popularity was fine, but in her view it was better earned in a working ambience than on a once-a-year basis! But only a few moments later, as she sipped her Buck's Fizz and the band started a mambo, he approached them.

'Everything OK here, Mike?' His smile was for Mike Redway, his gaze lowering to assess the amount of drink on the table. 'Order anything extra you need, won't you?'

'Sure, Dagan,' Mike returned easily. He had never made a secret of his admiration for his immediate superior, but he was no sycophant, and Dagan knew and appreciated his support, which was genuine and total.

Dagan's charming smile flicked round the table, encompassing them all, as Tamar felt herself stiffen in anticipation, her pulse quickening. This would be the moment he would ask her to dance. She'd worked with him for just over three months, been mentally and physically close to him, but apart from an accidental brushing of hands or touching of fingers she had never really touched or been touched by him.

She swallowed, her mouth unusually dry as she realised with a painful shock she was experiencing a strong yearning to be held in his arms, to move in the intimate circle of his embrace as their bodies translated the insidious beat filling the room.

She hadn't realised she'd clenched her hands in a purely nervous reaction, or that she'd primed herself to rise easily from her chair when he asked her. She just knew a sickening wave of disappointment when his sparkling glance came to rest on Simon.

'I wonder if I might have your permission to ask my secretary for a dance?'

'Of course,' mumbled Simon, as Pamela, her face pink with pleasure, pushed her chair back and allowed Dagan to lead her on to the floor.

Neil was chatting earnestly to Mike Redway, whose wife had disappeared to the powder-room as the other couples followed Dagan and Pamela. Only Simon sat staring glumly at his full glass.

Why did she feel so hurt and angry? Of course Pamela *was* his secretary. A junior secretary—but no one would have expected him to address her as that. Was she being unreasonable to expect that he would have asked her, Tamar, first? Yes, she was, she admitted. She had never pulled rank in her life, and the whole point of an office party was informality. There was no hierarchy that said Dagan was obliged to give her preference for his favours. Nevertheless she felt slighted, disappointed and angry.

A sudden thought struck her. Had Dagan at last examined his shopping and decided to show his displeasure by giving her a public snub? But no, she pacified herself, he'd smiled at her as warmly as at everyone else.

The word 'jealousy' edged its way into her mind, to be immediately rejected. To be jealous one had to be emotionally involved. That was something she would never allow herself to become with Dagan Carmichael. She shuddered, remembering that other office party so many years ago when she'd had the painful crush on

Martin Sanders that had ended in degradation and embarrassment. Her jaw tautened in resolution. She had made a fool of herself once, mistaking a powerful physical attraction for genuine emotion—it would never happen again.

CHAPTER FOUR

THE RHYTHM changed to the catchy beat of the cha-cha, several couples dropping out laughing and exhausted as the beat quickened, until only about a dozen remained, including Dagan and Pamela. The latter, face flushed, her young trim body full of energy, began to dance some of the more intricate variations, while Dagan provided a more inhibited foil to her gyrations. Gradually, as Tamar watched, the other couples drew aside, until by the time the music climaxed to a halt Pamela and her partner held centre stage. As the music stopped there was a spontaneous burst of applause, not only from the other couples who had given them the stage, but people at the surrounding tables who had stopped talking to observe the performance. Grinning, Dagan put his arm lightly on Pam's shoulder and guided her back to the table.

Burning with an incomprehensible resentment, Tamar heard her voice sounding critical and superior to her own ears. 'Cabaret as well this year!' she remarked cuttingly. She had spoken softly, but Dagan's ears were sharp.

'A popular one, too, judging from the applause.' He paused, having pulled Pam's chair out so that she could re-seat herself. He now stood, his hand resting lightly on her shoulder to meet Tamar's gaze across the table. There was a certain smugness in his tone which irritated her, but his narrowed eyes held a warning, if she had cared to read it.

'Of course,' she said coolly, a derisive little smile playing across her lips. 'One doesn't boo one's chief executive at Christmas if one still wants a job in the New Year!'

She didn't care much for the hardness glittering behind the blue stare, or the way his jaw tightened.

'You're a cynic, Miss Phillipson.' His unsmiling gaze locked with hers for a burning second before he turned away.

To anyone else at the table it might have sounded like playful repartee, but Tamar knew better. She had dared to prod the Dragon, and been rewarded by a tongue of fire. Small it might have been, but it had made her smart. Unaccountably she felt tears of chagrin rise up behind her eyes. Blinking them away, she rose to her feet, picking up her evening bag, forcing herself to stay composed as she walked to the sanctuary of the powder-room.

A few minutes later she was seated in its opulence, staring at her flushed face in the mirror, a feeling of aching emptiness somewhere in the region of her midriff. How could she have been so petty? She would have liked to blame her behaviour on the champagne content of the Buck's Fizz, but in her heart she knew it sprang from some deep-seated frustration of which Dagan Carmichael was at the core. Perhaps she was simply allergic to the man? He certainly had some strange effects on her—fast pulse-rate, flushed cheeks, trembling limbs—they must be symptoms of something.

After ten minutes she ventured back into the banqueting hall, her make-up restored to its meticulous best, unbearably relieved to see that Dagan had disappeared from their table.

Twice during the evening he returned, once to dance with Linda and a second time to partner Mike's wife.

On each occasion Tamar carefully avoided having to look at him, pretending to be deeply engrossed in conversation with Neil. She hardly expected an invitation to dance now, but she wouldn't give Dagan the satisfaction of seeing she'd even noticed his total disregard of her presence, or let him have a glimmer of an idea how much his lack of interest had hurt her.

When the last waltz was announced she turned warmly into Neil's arms, allowing him to gather her warm body hard against his own. His cheek lowered to rest against hers as his arm tightened on her waist, then moved to enjoy the easy undulation of her hips. Lifting her arms, she clasped them round Neil's neck, feeling a moment of disquiet as she sensed the arousal that flooded through him at her very close proximity. Almost against her will she stole a glance at the directors' table. Dagan was staring at her with unabashed interest, a wry twist to his mouth, and a strange glint in his narrowed eyes.

Quickly Tamar lowered her lashes, masking her curiosity. Heaven knew why she had wanted to look at him. She started as Neil's lips nibbled at her ear and then planted a kiss on her neck. Around them, everyone was behaving similarly, full of seasonal conviviality. There was no need to be priggish and call a halt to Neil's attentions, but she would have to be careful not to encourage him too far with her compliance. His reaction to her was so far removed from her own feelings, she felt a little guilty. Perhaps by the time he'd got his car out of the car park, and she'd kept him waiting while she collected her wrap from the cloakroom, his blood would have cooled down, she comforted herself optimistically, determining to be quite adamant about not inviting him in for coffee when he took her home.

She was so engrossed in her plans for getting rid of him without having to pretend to a passion she didn't feel, she wasn't aware that the last strains of the waltz had faded until he kissed her full on the lips.

'Hurry up and get your wrap, darling.' His voice was husky as he gave her an intimate little slap where the scarlet ruching graced her shapely rump. 'I can't wait to get you home.'

Tossing him a bright smile, she eased herself from his loving grasp, heading briskly for the cloakroom and taking as long as she dared before making her way down to the vast reception area of the hotel where she had arranged to meet him outside the jewellery display case. There was no sign of him, although owing to the length of time she had taken most of the crowd had already dispersed.

Biting her lip in concern, she moved towards the rendezvous, her black angora stole over her arm. Had Neil sensed her reticence and paid her back by driving off without her? He wasn't normally vengeful, but if he'd found the evening as disquieting as she had . . .

She thrust her worry to one side. If he didn't arrive within the next ten minutes, she would get herself a cab and hang the expense! What with one thing and another, what had started as a promising evening had left her feeling depleted and miserable.

'You certainly took your time, but I must admit the result was worth it!' The deep, unmistakable tones of Dagan Carmichael sounded right behind her as his hand came to rest in a light caress on her bare shoulder.

'I—I'm waiting for Neil,' she told him stiffly, masking her sense of shock at his proximity, and finding herself unable to meet his eyes.

'Yes, I know. He asked me to make you his apologies. Terry Lester's taking him on to Cortisi's.' Tamar's eyes widened at the mention of a private, very expensive gambling club. 'Stag only, I'm afraid.' Dagan's broad shoulders shrugged in their superbly styled dinner-jacket. 'Naturally he wouldn't have left you unprovided for, but I persuaded him I'd taken you home before and your welfare could safely be entrusted to my care.'

Anger at his high-handedness eliminated embarrassment at his presence. 'I'll get a taxi, then!'

'Don't be stupid, Tammy,' he said drily. 'My car's right outside.'

She allowed him to lead her to the forecourt, her momentary hope that he might be chauffeur-driven dispelled when she saw the Rover standing empty. Her body stiffened in defiance and she received a quick glance. 'Don't worry, I very seldom drink a lot, and hardly anything when I'm driving. I'm quite within the legal limits.'

He had misread her apprehension and she was thankful for it. The truth was, her feelings towards him were so mixed, his proximity so disturbing, she just wanted to be miles away from him, not sharing a car to south London.

Knowing when she was beaten, she took her place in the front passenger seat, holding herself rigid while he put the seat-belt round her, grateful when his fingers, lean and efficient, avoided direct contact with her body.

As he moved the car into the street, she stole a glance at his strong profile, evaluating the straight nose, passionate, tender mouth with its shorter top lip, the rounded aggressive chin and lean, hard-boned jaw. A heady mixture on the eye. A face men would acknowledge as personable and women call handsome.

'I suppose *you* arranged this visit to Cortisi's?'

It was the obvious conclusion to draw. From what she knew about Terry, the club was well outside his reach.

'That's right,' Dagan agreed smoothly, not taking his eyes off the road. 'I'm toying with the idea of letting Lester handle the negotiations for this new electronics interest of theirs.'

'But Mike services Hathaway Childs,' she protested disbelievingly. 'You're surely not going to take a plum like that away from Mike!'

She saw the corner of his mouth twitch, the quick blink of dark lashes.

'I might let them share it. It's a progressive agency, with enough clients to merit two representatives, and Lester will have time on his hands now I've taken him off Fulhams.'

'You've taken Terry off Fulhams just because they're handling Creta and he's missed out!' The unfairness of it shook her. To lose a large agency like that would be considered a demotion by his contemporaries, and it was hardly Terry's fault that the representative of their rivals was a nubile female. 'But someone's got to represent us there, and I can't think of anyone better than Terry in normal circumstances!' she protested, stung by what she saw as a cruel and retributive decision.

'No?' The corner of Dagan's mouth quirked. 'But the present circumstances are far from normal, and you know what they say—one must fight fire with fire.' He turned his head, slightly smiling at her outraged face. 'I've given the job to Fiamma.'

'Fiamma!' Tamar nearly choked. Fiamma Doyle had only recently joined INI, being one of Dagan's first appointments. In her late twenties, she was a striking redhead, slim as a rake with a translucent complexion and a restless vitality which hinted at a super-active thyroid input.

Trained as an actress, but never achieving leading roles, she had decided to enter the world of advertisement repping and had joined INI in that capacity in the classified department. Everyone liked her. Her infectious, slightly ribald sense of humour was much appreciated, and her undoubted sex appeal had made her an outright winner with the male staff—but to promote her from the relative obscurity of classified to the eminence of handling a prestige agency like Fulhams was an astonishing and unprecedented action.

'You obviously don't approve,' the man at her side said mildly, as Tamar's shock showed on her expressive face.

'It's hardly up to me to comment,' she told him coolly. 'Doubtless you had your reasons, and I can scarcely believe your sole motivation was to persuade her to wean the account director's affections away from his present love.'

'Well, I suppose I should be grateful you've given me the benefit of the doubt, and you're quite right. I haven't yet stooped to pimping on the company's behalf.' There was no denying the acidity of his tone as he continued briskly, 'I intend Fiamma to introduce herself direct to the client—the advertisement director of Creta itself. Since she's new to the job I'm hoping he'll have the courtesy to see her. After that, it's up to her. But the time for facts and figures is long past. On paper INI deserve at least half the budget, and it's in Creta's own interests to spread their campaign to include both media groups. Fiamma is an attractive girl with a sparkling personality. In my opinion, if anyone can swing the pendulum back in our direction, she can.'

It was a bold and imaginative stroke, Tamar had to admit, and as a last resort she supposed it stood as much chance as any other. She turned her head to gaze out of the side window, wondering why Dagan had chosen that moment to confide in her. He could hardly be truly interested in her opinion, could he?

She was conscious of his amused glance dwelling on the back of her head. 'You know, with your hair up like that you remind me of the first time we met,' he confided softly.

'When you mistook me for the cleaner?' she asked icily, looking down her short straight nose at him. 'That's not the prettiest compliment I've received this evening.'

His deep laughter echoed in the close confines of the car. 'I'm sure it's not,' he agreed. 'What I meant was it gives you a look of haughty disdain—not that it was unattractive. Or is it just being in my company socially that makes the ice run in your veins?'

'I don't know what you mean,' she said flatly, tensing as he drew up at a set of traffic lights and took the opportunity to regard her at leisure, an amused quirk turning the corners of his strong mouth.

'Oh, but I'm sure you do,' he contradicted her, restarting the engine as the lights changed. 'Am I expected to apologise for depriving you of your lover's company this evening? I can assure you I didn't twist his arm, so perhaps you should be blaming him instead for being prepared to forsake you in favour of a more fickle mistress.'

'What exactly are you insinuating?' Anger flamed her cheeks with a smudge of scarlet.

He shrugged. 'Nothing more than that, according to appearances on the dance-floor before you left, Hathaway was staking a very strong claim to enjoy your company for the remainder of the night—or should I say morning?—and wasn't being discouraged.' This close to him, she could see the slightly enigmatic twist of his lips. 'Don't sound so outraged, Tammy. I'm no moralist. I was merely making an observation—not a criticism.'

Tamar swallowed hard, painfully aware that her own compliant behaviour in Neil's arms had given a false impression of her intentions. Yet wasn't that exactly what she'd meant to do? To show Dagan Carmichael that she hadn't needed his attention at the party to ensure her thorough enjoyment of the proceedings? Now, with Neil's defection, the whole thing had backfired on her. Instead of her appearing *soignée* and desirable, Dagan's interference had cast her in the role of the deserted sweetheart, doing nothing to reinstate her value in his eyes.

As her temper spurted, she smothered a defiant urge to ask him to stop the car and let her out—caution warning her that he might just be awkward enough to obey, and then she would be well and truly stranded. Besides, it was absurd to feel hurt because he assumed she and Neil were lovers. In the world they both frequented, people hopped in and out of bed with each other with boring regularity and infinite variety. To have imagined he saw her as any more selective was wishful thinking.

Striving to retain some dignity, she raised a delicately arched eyebrow, saying frostily, 'My plans for this evening are hardly your business.'

'Only in as much as I seem to have ruined them,' he remarked calmly, apparently in no way quelled by her lack of warmth. 'I'm afraid we can't join Hathaway and

Lester, but perhaps you'd care to go on to a nightclub? I know of several where we...'

The last thing she needed was his pity! Her heavy sigh interrupted him mid-sentence. 'No, thank you all the same, Dagan. The only thing I want to do now is go home to bed.' Embarrassment burned her cheeks as she saw Dagan's smile and realised the interpretation that could be put on her unthinking remark. Stolidly she continued, ignoring the unwitting *double entendre*, 'I have to catch an early train for Bournemouth in the morning, and I haven't even started packing yet.'

To her relief, the dark head inclined slightly. 'Then home and bed it is, Tammy.'

Tamar sat silently as the powerful car surged along the quiet streets. Whatever was the matter with her? Why was she experiencing such ambivalent feelings towards the man at her side? It couldn't be because of Neil. As far as that was concerned, she should be grateful she'd been saved the embarrassment of telling the younger man that she hadn't changed her mind about having an affair with him.

True, Dagan's action had been high-handed, especially in view of his suspicions, but he *was* going to the trouble of taking her home, even though it was on his own way to Surrey. She glanced from beneath lowered lashes at the strong profile beside her, feeling her pulse gather momentum. What was it about him that could make her senses reel? At first she had put it down to a nervous excitement about working for a new boss, and one with such a dynamic reputation, but during the past three months it was clear their business association, although not without its contretemps, was highly successful...or at least, that was what she *had* been thinking.

Recently she had sensed a change in his attitude towards her, which was difficult to evaluate. For one thing, although Pamela had received a seven-pound box of hand-made chocolates from him as a Christmas present, she herself had received nothing. There was, of course, no reason why he should buy her a gift, although it was traditional that managers and directors did give their personal staff some token of appreciation.

Hugh Drummond had always bought her a scarf, she recalled with a rueful smile, remembering how her stocking drawer still harboured the fruits of his shopping labours. As they said, it was the thought that counted. And Dagan hadn't even spared her that.

Dear heavens, how she detested the man! For ignoring her all evening, for daring to whip Neil away from her side, but most of all because just the fact of his sitting so close to her, controlling the powerful car with easy authority, had aroused a thrumming vibration through the length of her body from the quickened pulse in her throat to the uneasy tautness of her shapely calf muscles, and she wished with all her heart for the journey to end quickly, so that she could be released from the uncomfortable magnetism he was exerting over her.

Thankful to arrive at her destination, she was surprised when Dagan took the Yale key from her, opening the front door with a slick turn of his wrist. Keeping his fingers on the key, he pushed the door open, allowing her to enter. Before she knew quite how it had happened, they were standing facing each other at the foot of the stairs leading to her first-floor apartment, the door firmly closed behind them.

'Thank you for the lift.' She forced a cool smile to lips which were strangely warm and dry. 'You'll forgive me if I don't invite you up for coffee, but it's very late and, as I said, I have to make an early start in the morning.'

'Well, coffee wasn't a major part of my plan, Tammy,' Dagan returned gravely, making no attempt to take his leave, and she felt a wave of sick excitement rise from somewhere deep inside her at the dangerous glint behind his ridiculously thick sweep of eyelashes. They were the only vaguely feminine feature on that hard, masculine face, and they made his vibrant masculinity all the greater by contrast.

Since her earlier indiscretion, Tammy had cultivated a reserve of coolness which had enabled her to keep predatory men in their place. Most of them looking for an office flirtation were easily discouraged by her obvious lack of interest. Neil had been the exception, but then he had none of the brutal attraction for her which had made her such a fall-over for the meretricious charm of Martin Sanders, so she had felt safe enough to allow herself to unbend a little. But there was no sign that Dagan was impressed by her assumed indifference. She couldn't even be sure what thoughts were passing through his head at that moment, but from the wicked expression in those dark blue eyes she guessed they boded little good for her.

Uncertainty glazed her eyes, as she acknowledged weakly that a strong inner voice was prompting her to allow him to stay for just a few more minutes—if that was what he wanted.

'Scared, Tammy?' he mocked softly. 'And well you might be! You and I have some unfinished business to discuss. Will you lead the way—or shall I?' He nodded towards the stairs, but made no movement in their direction. Perhaps if she repeated her refusal now he would leave as requested... Whether it was his unyielding air of command or her extensive training to compliance as a secretary she didn't know, but she heard her voice shake slightly as she said resignedly, 'Well, only ten minutes, then,' and led the way upstairs.

'This is nice!' Dagan passed an appreciative look round the pleasant lounge-cum-dining-room as she snapped the centre light on. 'Must be expensive to run.'

'I pay for it myself, if that's what you mean!' she responded sharply, determined to quash any insinuation that someone else might be subsidising her rent. 'After all, you pay me a good salary.'

But his surprise was understandable, she allowed. If her widowed mother hadn't given each of her two daughters a substantial sum of money on the sale of her house in Westcliff prior to moving to Bournemouth to live with her elder daughter and family, she would never have been able to live as graciously as she did. But she wasn't prepared to discuss her private life with Dagan. What interest could it possibly hold for a man of his diverse interests?

'Don't be so bristly, Tammy,' he reproved, prowling over to an elegant teak bureau to switch on a soft rose-shaded table-lamp, standing back to admire it for a moment while she watched him in mounting exasperation.

'Dagan, please—' she remonstrated. 'You said something about unfinished business. Surely I didn't forget anything yesterday—or is it something to do with Creta?'

'Don't be impatient.' His approving glance drifted over her tautly held body. 'The business I spoke of was personal—but first things first.'

He was back at the door, raising his hand to flick off the centre light, leaving the room palely illuminated in a rosy glow.

'Now—' he said, his deep tone oozing with satisfaction. Before she had even realised what he meant to do, he was back in front of her, sliding his arms around her, finding her startled lips with his own.

A warm weakness flooded her body, flowing through her muscles as her mouth yielded without reservation to the growing demands made upon it. Boneless in his arms, Tammy was no longer capable of conscious thought as Dagan, sensing her lack of resistance, drew her even closer to himself, sending delicious tremors of arousal singing through her so that instinctively she eased her soft form into his, a mounting fever within her forcing her to savour the muscled hardness that confronted her, to enjoy the feel of Dagan's long, hard thighs tense beneath the elegant black cloth that cloaked their animal power with a veneer of civilisation.

'Tammy?' He breathed her name, half caress, half question, as he released her tingling mouth to carry the warmth of his lips across her cheek, his voice soft and husky in her ear. 'I've been wanting to do that all evening.'

'Have you?' She stared into the midnight blue of his eyes, and read the unmistakable glaze of desire softening the dark pupils as an answering ache stirred deep inside her, and she admitted to herself that it was what she'd wanted too. But with her it went back further than the start of the evening. Deep in her subconscious mind, the thought stirred that she had wanted to experience the pleasure of being in Dagan's arms ever since that first day when he had walked half-naked from the bathroom, but now for the first time she was honest enough to recognise and admit it. She pushed the thought away. The days of her immaturity when she'd responded with her body rather than her mind were long in the past.

'Ah...' He smiled at her uncertain expression. 'You're wondering why I didn't ask you for a dance, hmm? The answer to that one's quite simple. I was working on the principle that the guy who gets the last waltz takes the lady home, but when the time came you made quite certain that wasn't going to be my privilege—so I was forced to take other measures.'

'You sent Neil off with Terry Lester on my behalf?' Already she was succumbing to the erotic mixture of aftershave and the warm, aroused skin scent of a healthy adult male, allied to the subtle pressure of Dagan's body as it impressed its predatory form against her.

There was cool laughter in the eyes that met her uncertain gaze. 'Let's say I brought my plans forward a little. One has to be adaptable in this business.'

'I'm sure,' she acknowledged a trifle breathlessly. Cool, she must keep cool and not over-react. What was a Christmas kiss between two people who worked closely together? As long as she didn't encourage Dagan any further, there was no harm done. Raising her hands to his chest, she gave a little push, intent on breaking his embrace, but when he let out a sigh of obvious pleasure at the touch of her palms against the crispness of his shirt she moved her hands rapidly to rest on his arms, glad to escape the heavy thunder of his heart beneath her fingers.

Every nerve-ending in her body was quivering with a need she had never guessed at before as he repossessed her dubious mouth, teasing and flirting with a sweet sensuousness that made her toes curl with pleasure and started a strange spiral of desire spinning upwards to her throat and downwards until its intensity forced her to realise what was happening to her.

As panic tightened her throat, she moved uneasily, unhappily aware of Dagan's very fast, very male reaction to her proximity and the problems it was creating in her own body. Dear heaven—as Dagan's strong, smooth hands travelled across the firm skin of her naked back, she was as powerless to control the yawning ache of her muscles and the staccato pulses at her throat and wrists as she would have been to control an attack of hiccups. Somehow she didn't think holding her breath was going to help, either!

Yet she knew she had to stop the heady build-up of physical awakening that could be leading in only one direction. Even without the lingering memory of the misery she had suffered the last time she had given in to her baser instincts, it was against all her principles to become involved with someone she worked with. In a few days she would have to face Dagan across an office desk, and she wanted to be able to do so without embarrassment.

Gathering all her will-power, she expelled him gently but firmly from her mouth, and he accepted the decision reluctantly, trying to make her relent before finally allowing her to win the battle, only to seek her neck with his strong, soft mouth.

Taking her courage in both hands, she pushed his face away, hoping he couldn't feel how she shivered to feel his warm satin skin, with its underlying growth of dark hair already beginning to break the surface, beneath her fingers.

Now was the time to appear *blasé,* as if she often indulged in such amorous pursuits, and to hide from Dagan exactly how disturbing she found him.

'Your ten minutes is up, sir,' she said pertly, hoping she sounded sophisticated and determined. 'I'll have to ask you to leave.'

CHAPTER FIVE

TAMAR was breathing unevenly, tendrils of her hair drifting down from the diamanté clasp which had confined them. All she could feel now was dismay that she had encouraged him, and a mounting fear that he might not take his dismissal so easily. Martin Sanders' furious face, bloated with unsatiated desire, floated before her mind's eye, and she cringed, recalling the blow he had struck at her. But on that occasion she had gone much further down the road towards consummation. Surely Dagan would accept her withdrawal without recrimination—or had he expected her to take him to her bed? The same bed that he obviously believed she shared with Neil?

Her heart beat faster as a frown darkened his brow, and for a moment she thought he was about to accuse her angrily of leading him on. Tearing herself away from his loosened clasp, her face paling with anguish, she backed away from him.

'For heaven's sake, Tammy!' His harsh retort did nothing to lessen her fears. 'Don't look at me like that. I know my temper can be a bit uncertain, but it's hardly flattering to be looked at as if I were a rapist or a murderer!'

He looked so wounded, a slightly hysterical laugh escaped her lips, as she felt her tension lessen.

'I'm sorry, Dagan.' A nervous smile touched her mouth. 'It's just that I'm rather tired and a little overwrought. I didn't mean to give you the impression that

I'd...' She hesitated, her luminous grey eyes uncon-
sciously pleading for him not to take umbrage as she
sought for a suitable word to express her feelings.

'Jump into bed with me on our first date?' he
suggested softly, a glimmer of a smile shadowing his
mouth, as he saw the delicate flush rise beneath her pale
skin. 'No, you didn't do that, although I'd be a liar if
I said I wouldn't have accepted such an offer with alacrity
and much pleasure.'

'Yes, well...' She fought to regain her composure,
grateful for his understanding, but her nerves prickling
uneasily at the soft mockery of his tone. 'It wasn't exactly
a date either, was it?'

'Unfortunately, no—but the next time we have dinner
together will be.'

'That's very kind of you...' She saw his eyebrows lift
at her repressive tone, but struggled on regardless. 'But
I've always made it a practice not to date anyone who
works for the same company.'

'An excellent policy,' he returned warmly, much to
her surprise. 'That gives me the consolation of knowing
I have no rivals among my own staff. I should hate to
start the New Year by having to dismiss someone who'd
already gained your favours!' He turned and walked
leisurely towards the long chintz-covered settee in the
window bay, sitting down, legs sprawled in front of him.
'And now, how about that cup of coffee you promised
me?'

Tamar was half-way to the kitchen, laughter trembling on her lips at his insouciant reply, when she realised she had most definitely not invited him for coffee.
Still, now the tension between them had dwindled away,
there would be no harm in providing him with a cup.

Moments later he accepted from her hand the bone-china mug with its fragrant brew with a nod of thanks. 'Now for the business I mentioned earlier,' he said briskly as she took her own seat in an armchair facing him. 'I owe you for the shopping you got on my behalf.'

'No,' Tamar was taken unawares, surprise reflected on her face. 'I took the money from petty cash and you settled at the end of the week.'

'That's not quite what I meant, is it, Tammy?' A muscle spasmed in his cheek, and despite the solemnity of his blue gaze she sensed the hidden amusement inside him.

Realisation dawned as a shamefaced smile parted her pretty mouth. 'I guess I do owe you an apology. They *were* awful, weren't they?'

'Dreadful,' he agreed instantly, his face set in stern lines. 'I must say I was surprised at Neil Hathaway's taste.'

The allusion didn't escape her. He had asked her to get what her boyfriend wore or what pleased her. Well, she certainly wasn't going to tell him she had no idea what underwear Neil favoured, since their relationship hadn't progressed to such a degree of intimacy. Instead she made a deprecating movement of her hands, saying tritely, 'There's no accounting for taste.'

'Obviously not.' He took a tentative sip of coffee. '"Get lost" and a maple leaf,' he mused, to her continuing discomfort. 'Was that your way of saying—Canada go home?'

'No!' Tamar denied the surmise quickly, a little shocked that he should have sought a deeper meaning for what had been meant as a light-hearted hint that he should buy his own personal items. True, she had first judged him as a rash intruder into her comfortable, well-oiled working life, but over the past few weeks that opinion had been revised by his obvious talent for the job and a consideration for loyal members of staff she hadn't at first assumed him capable of. Far from Dagan being the hatchet-man of his reputation, his first few weeks at INI had shown him to be more of an expert gardener—pruning away the dead wood, encouraging new shoots to establish themselves, fertilising the barren ground of lost opportunities with a sprinkling of optimism and stimulation. Tamar smiled secretly at her own whimsy as he nodded with satisfaction.

'That's all right, then. Because as a matter of fact I'm as British as you are. My roots go back to Wales— although I must admit it's some time since I last walked in the valleys.'

'Wales?' For a moment surprise held her silent. Somehow she had always believed his drive and ambition were peculiarly North American, then she said with a laugh, 'Where else? The ancient land of dragons!'

'True.' He acknowledged the implicit reference to his nickname before leaning back and closing his eyes. 'Did you know that damned maple leaf was fluorescent in the dark?'

'Oh, no!' Tamar choked in horror, her body beginning to tremble with mounting laughter at the graphic picture his words conjured up. 'Oh, Dagan! It was a rotten trick played in a moment of annoyance. I truly am sorry.'

'Then I shall expect you to prove it with a suitable penance when I choose to exact one.' Carefully he placed his mug on a nearby table and rose to his feet. 'And now, before I go and leave you to your dreams, there's just one more thing.' His hand slid inside his jacket to produce a small box. 'Happy Christmas, Tammy, and thank you for all the hard work you've put in over the past weeks.'

He hadn't forgotten her! Pleasure welled through Tamar's whole being as she accepted the plain, un-wrapped jeweller's box, her fingers shaking a little as she opened the lid to gaze down on a gold brooch fash-ioned in the shape of a dragonfly. Delicate and beau-tiful, it perched on a bed of white satin, a slender box chain trailed around it.

'I wasn't sure if you'd prefer a brooch or a necklace,' his deep voice was saying somewhere near her as she stared speechless at the gift. 'And I preferred not to ask Pamela, so I chose the best of both worlds.'

It must have cost a fortune! It would be impossible to accept it. Yet it was beautiful and she wanted it, and the last thing she wanted to do was appear churlish. While she stood in silent anguish, Dagan took the box from her nerveless hands, threaded the chain through the clasp of the brooch and, moving behind her, strung the golden creature round her neck. 'There!' he said triumphantly. 'Yes, it looks as good as I'd hoped.'

'Dagan...' She turned to face him. 'I don't know what to say...'

'"Thank you" will be quite sufficient,' he said kindly, as if she were an idiot.

'It's not the kind of gift a man gives to his secretary.' Her troubled eyes beseeched him to understand her dilemma.

'Not unless she's a very special secretary,' he agreed, his eyes soft and watchful. 'And he has hopes of per-suading her to become even more special in the future.'

Tamar's throat was dry and aching as she raised her hands to the back of her neck, seeking the elusive clasp. 'I meant what I said, Dagan,' she said huskily. 'I enjoy working for you, but only if we can keep it on an impersonal level.'

'Why?' He was toughly contentious now, his underlying ruthlessness evident. 'A few moments ago you were anything but impersonal in my arms. Over the past weeks I pride myself I've come to know you very well. You're the personification of discretion, my Tammy, and I've no doubt that you can keep your personal and professional life apart in the office, if you so choose.'

'Not if you're suggesting we have an affair. It would be an impossible situation,' she insisted stubbornly, determined to leave him under no false impressions, although she could do nothing to control the curl of excitement that unfolded inside her at the very thought of having Dagan Carmichael as a lover.

He gave a harsh laugh. 'Half the managers in INI sleep with their secretaries!'

It was an exaggeration, but not without foundation, and she wasn't going to contest it, merely comment on it.

'And it almost always ends in tears for the girl concerned. She loses both her pride and her job when her lover turns elsewhere, as he inevitably does! Believe me, I've seen it happen more than once.' She confronted him defiantly, fighting down her inner turbulence.

'I said you were a cynic...' After a few silent seconds Dagan sighed, a reluctant smile softening his hard face, as he put his hand beneath her chin. 'Don't worry, Tammy. I shan't let the fact that I want you interfere with my business acumen, or make life difficult for you in working hours. Neither is your present anything but a token of gratitude for your services in the past. So give me a thank-you kiss and we'll let the New Year look after itself.'

He lowered his head and brushed his lips gently across hers, before stepping back to straighten the immaculate line of his evening suit. 'I'll see myself out.'

In a daze Tamar followed him to the door, watching him walk down the stairs, feeling as if she had been put through a wringer. At the door he turned, looking up at her. 'Don't be too late on Thursday, will you? We're still chasing half a million!'

Standing in the dim glow of the main room, she heard the Rover's engine purr into life, before walking to the mirror and staring at her reflection.

Carefully she undid the glistening clasp that confined her hair, allowing it to fall about her face. Whatever happened now, her life would never be the same again. She *did* think it was disastrous for a secretary to allow her boss to become her lover. The experiences of other girls over the previous years had shown her that few emerged unscathed from such an association. But it wasn't only that. It was Dagan himself. Her initial hostility towards him had died, but she hated the kind of social life he reputedly enjoyed—using women for his physical comfort and pleasure, without commitment or love. She had no intention of finding her name added to the list already gracing his diary.

Her fingers caressed the graceful contours of the dragonfly. It surely wasn't coincidence that he had chosen something so redolent of his own nickname. She shivered, recalling the touch of his mouth on the hollow of her neck where the graceful brooch rested.

It would be foolish to deny the chemistry between them, but there was no way she would go to bed with a man unless she loved him. Hadn't she found out the hard way that physical attraction alone wasn't enough? For one dreadful moment earlier that evening she had feared that history was to repeat itself, that Dagan, frustrated and angry, would do to her what Martin had done—attempt to take her without a word of love or any kind of preliminary caress because she had been stupid enough to mistake her admiration of his good looks as a substitute for loving him.

She had been eighteen at the time, and a very immature eighteen at that, working in London on her first job, and when Martin had chosen her to accompany him to a party she had been over the moon. Later, when he had persuaded her to go back to his flat, she had told herself it was the modern thing to do, and, stupidly believing that she loved him, had allowed him to take her to bed.

Even now, six years later, the memory of what had followed was a nightmare. She had realised within a few seconds that she had made a terrible mistake, that Martin, despite his pretty compliments, cared nothing for her. She had felt guilty for misunderstanding him, and too unsophisticated and afraid to tell him she had changed her mind, believing she deserved to endure the results of her own stupidity.

Perhaps if he had been a considerate lover, the trauma she had suffered would have been less; but he hadn't been, and it wasn't. Her frightened and unloved body had adamantly refused to admit him into its inner sanctum, and he had grown angrier and more violent as she had dissolved into bitter tears of shame and pain. Finally her ordeal had ended when he had left her, striking a blow across her mouth as a parting gift to demonstrate his opinion of what he termed 'a teasing little tart.'

She had left the company, of course. Even without the vicious stories he put about that had other men giving her sly winks and her erstwhile friends in the typing pool giggling, she would have gone. There was no way she could have worked anywhere near him.

For a while afterwards she'd thought of herself as frigid, until common sense had come to her rescue. She had been young and incredibly stupid, but she'd learned a valuable lesson. No longer would she envy her more permissive friends with their shoals of boyfriends. She would wait for a man who would love her as much as she loved him. And when she did fall in love it wouldn't be with some handsome entrepreneur or a man like her own father, who had roamed the world as an engineer going from oil installation to oil installation, leaving her mother to cope with her two young daughters until the fatal accident which had left her a widow with two young children to support unaided. No, it would be with a quiet, respectable, genuine man who worked from nine till five and played golf on Sundays!

She tossed her head, as if shaking off unhappy memories. What she had felt for Dagan was physical attraction—a chemistry she had recognised subconsciously from the first time they had met. Now she was aware of its full danger, she could combat it. If necessary, she would accept more of Neil's invitations, to illustrate her lack of interest in Dagan's proposal, since Neil was a far less potent danger to her resolve.

As for Dagan Carmichael... As if drawn by a power outside her control, her fingers rose to touch the golden necklet. He was a man with his eye on the main chance, and a diary full of dates. He would hardly be devastated by her decision not to join his harem!

Inside the office, she would continue to give him her expert and unstinted assistance at all times. Outside the office, he wouldn't exist for her.

*   *   *

It had been a damp, mild Christmas, and Tamar's train arrived back at Waterloo on schedule, enabling her to get a cab without difficulty and to be in her office on time. Despite Dagan's concession, it had been a matter of pride not to take the extra hours he had been prepared to give her. Since she had decided to keep their relationship on a strictly business basis, it would be unethical of her to accept favours from him.

To be honest, she was dreading their first meeting. Would Dagan have regretted his amorous approach, and show it by treating her with a cool disdain, or worse still, would he greet her with some kind of embarrassing innuendo? Nervously she smoothed down the skirt of the new pale blue lambswool jumper and skirt suit she was wearing, suddenly uncomfortably aware of the shortness of its fashionable skirt. It had been her sister's Christmas present to her and she'd taken the first opportunity of wearing it. Now she wished she had chosen something that didn't draw attention to the long, shapely length of her nylon-clad legs. She would hate Dagan to imagine she'd gone out of her way to emphasise her feminine attributes.

Damn it, she thought crossly, annoyed at the untypical confusion of her thoughts. She would just have to keep her fingers crossed that those few minutes of mindless pleasure she had shared with him hadn't destroyed a working relationship that had grown so satisfying during the past months.

She started guiltily as the door to her office opened.

'You made it on time, then?' Dagan's smile was totally disarming, relaxing her tension instantly, as he walked into the room. It was just as if nothing untoward had happened between them at all: only the sudden fillip of her heart taking her by surprise. She actually felt her taut muscles loosen as she followed him into his office.

'Did you have a good holiday? Everything all right with your family?' he asked pleasantly, shrugging off his heavy jacket and opening the wardrobe to place it out of sight.

'Yes, they're all fine,' she answered truthfully. 'And it was a nice traditional family celebration.' She hesitated a second before asking as politeness dictated, 'I hope you had a good time, too?'

'Mmm,' he said absently, returning to his desk to pick up his diary. 'Fair enough.'

He was running his finger down the list of appointments she had extracted and typed out on a separate sheet for him. 'Good grief, Tammy, what's this one— Jenson Associates?' His brows furrowed in puzzlement as he stared at the sheet.

'They're handling this new cold cure, and want us to come up with some data to show our readers catch more colds than readers of *The Times* and the *Telegraph*,' she reminded him, repressing a smile at the blank shock mirrored on his good-looking face. 'Of course it's impossible. We did try to prove they spent more on cold cures per capita, but you said you'd call in and see the account director personally.'

'It must have been one of my off-days,' he muttered, grimacing at his own rashness. 'What's it worth to us?'

Tamar mentioned the size of the budget, then added, 'John Cavendish handles it, and he felt very strongly we could get our share, but the account director felt a bit aggrieved because he wasn't invited to the last presentation we held at the Mayfair.'

'Yeah, yeah,' Dagan passed lean fingers through his thick, dark hair, pondering the vanities of his associates, 'I remember it now.'

Tamar produced a large folder from one corner of his desk, saying crisply, 'Good. All the relevant details are in here. But it's really a personal visit they're hankering for.'

'Well, I suppose it's worth following up.' He glanced at his watch. 'See if Fiamma's in yet, will you, please, and ask her to come and see me right away? And as soon as anyone in editorial puts in an appearance, tell them I'm still waiting for copies of February's holiday features.'

He continued to reel off a list of things he wanted done as Tamar made the necessary notes, glad to see he was in his usual sparkling form and that apparently nothing had changed between them. She had read too much into a casual Christmas flirtation, she comforted herself happily. It was about time her sophistication grew in measure with her age!

It was on a Thursday two weeks later that she had cause to rethink her conclusion. Opening Dagan's personal diary, she saw her own name pencilled in for the following day. 'Dinner—Tamar,' the entry read, and it certainly hadn't been there yesterday! She stood frowning down at it. It was possible he knew another girl with the same name, but not probable. She looked up hesitantly to meet Dagan's faint smile as his dark eyes locked with her puzzled regard.

'It's rather short notice,' he said easily. 'I hope you can make it, but it can easily be postponed if you've made other arrangements. There's a very good little restaurant I've discovered not far from where I live, where we can have a quiet meal away from other media people.'

Tamar swallowed uneasily, her mind in a turmoil. If he had asked her out immediately after the holiday, she would have turned him down without hesitation, still full of an iron resolve not to mix business and pleasure, but he had lulled her with two weeks of total impartiality, and now he was presenting her with what appeared to be a *fait accompli*. In fact, he wasn't even giving her a choice of whether she would go out with him or not, merely a choice of dates!

'Thank you for the invitation,' she said coolly, 'but I'm afraid I can't accept it.'

'Name your date, then.' His dark brows lifted slightly. 'My diary's got ample space.'

It was something she had remarked for herself, as she'd turned the pristine pages of the new year, but the thought gave her no comfort, as she tried to find a way of making her point without being offensive.

'What I'm trying to say, Dagan, is that I don't think it's a good idea for me to see you outside working hours. It might give people the wrong impression.'

'What people? Neil Hathaway, you mean?' He looked at her, a slight smile playing about his well-formed mouth. 'Until you wear his ring, I'd say he had no grounds for monitoring your dinner dates.'

'Not Neil, particularly,' said Tamar uncomfortably. 'It's as I told you before. It's one of my principles never to go out with anyone who works for the same company. I just don't like being the subject of gossip, however innocent the outing.'

'Who said anything about it being innocent?' asked Dagan mildly, seemingly unaware of the colour that rose to Tamar's cheeks at the insinuation. 'It's a long time since anyone has referred to me in such terms. Still, I fail to see how your reputation as an ice maiden could

be ruined by joining me for a meal in a reputable restaurant. And I'm very much afraid I can't take no for
an answer. You have a penance to pay, Tammy, remember? And this is it. You said you were sorry about
your unfortunate purchases, and now I'm asking you to
prove it.'

He rose to his feet, strolling idly round the desk until
he was standing in front of her. Taking the diary from
her hands, he laid it down on the desk. 'You're not being
asked to enjoy my company—in fact, it would hardly
be a penance if you did, would it?' His touch on her
shoulder was as gentle as a butterfly alighting, yet it sent
a stream of fire surging down her arm as she tensed
against what his nearness could do to her.

To protest too much would betray her vulnerability.
After all, he was right, what harm could there be in going
out for a meal? And he had been careful to point out
that she was unlikely to be seen by anyone who knew
her. An evening with Dagan Carmichael, away from the
formality of the office...the pulse in her throat flut-
tered wildly. Dear heaven, what was the matter with her?
She was no teenager to be swept off her feet, and to
stand here dithering was to give the whole matter much
more importance than it deserved.

The sensible thing would be to pay her so-called
penance with dignity, and that would be that. Dagan
enjoyed winning, and to rob him of the satisfaction of
persuading her to act against her better judgement was
to spur him to find a more unpleasant penalty for her
to pay. She would humour the boyish stubbornness in
him this once; the incident need never be repeated!

'I'd like to know what thoughts are going on behind
those beautiful eyes of yours.' The hand was removed.
'If you look at me like that much longer, Miss Phillipson,

I shall be very tempted to kiss you, and that would never do. It's always been one of my most stringent principles never to make love to my secretary in the office.' He laughed as she stepped quickly away from him. Damn the man! He was mocking her, and she was doing nothing to dissuade him by staring at him as if he were about to seduce her.

She forced her shoulders into a negligent shrug. 'Very well, since I'm to be punished, I may as well get it over as quickly as possible. I can arrange to be free tomorrow.'

'Splendid!' he said blithely, pushing the diary towards her. 'Ink the entry in, then, will you, please, Tammy? And then we'll go through the post.'

It was, Tammy thought grimly, inscribing her own name as instructed, rather like being made to enter one's name in the punishment book at school. Did Dagan have any idea just what a strain he would be putting on her defences? Having seen his satisfied smirk at her capitulation, she rather thought he did. Well, forewarned was forearmed. She'd given in on this small point: but it was the only surrender she intended to make!

The following day she wore a royal blue woollen dress to work, conscious that its ribbed weave flattered her curves without being too clinging and it was as suitable for a day in the office as dining out afterwards. Searching for jewellery to complement it, she had found herself gazing at Dagan's gift, admiring for the hundredth time its delicate beauty, still uncomfortably aware that it implicitly requested favours she was totally unprepared to grant, despite the donor's insistence that it was for past help only. She would never have the courage to wear it in Dagan's presence—it would be like a signal of intentions she didn't have. Fortunately it would be totally unsuitable for wear with the dress she had chosen, so she was under no pressure to wear it for the sake of politeness. Eventually she had chosen simple, chunky accessories—matching gold and ivory bracelet and earrings.

Freshening up in Dagan's bathroom that evening, she reapplied her make-up with a steady hand, despite the butterflies fluttering about inside her. Normally she would have used the ladies' room further along the corridor, despite Dagan's casual assumption that she would share his private facilities. Somehow sharing a bathroom with him, even in an office ambience, gave her a feeling of an intimacy she preferred to steer away from. Besides, the ladies' room was a traditional meeting-place for the secretaries, and although Tamar had never 'dished the dirt' with the rest of the girls, she certainly was no snob and took her part in the brief and lively exchanges that took place there.

Tonight was different, though, because she had no wish to be questioned about her plans for the evening. To tell the truth was unthinkable, and to lie was to give too much importance to her date. Smoothly she worked in two shades of grey eyeshadow on her lids, and lengthened and thickened her naturally long lashes. In office hours she played down her eye make-up. The change was suitably dramatic, she noted with satisfaction, brushing a soft pink lipstick on to the full outlines of her pretty mouth, before completing her toilette by brushing her soft blonde hair away from her brow so that it fell into a shining complement round her oval face. Dagan was used to escorting some of the world's most beautiful and glamorous women, from all she had heard. She owed it to herself to present Tamar Phillipson in her best groomed condition!

If she had any doubt she'd succeeded, it would have been dispelled by Dagan's reaction as she emerged into his office, where he sat patiently waiting on the cream chesterfield. Rising to his feet, he surveyed her in silence for a full ten seconds, before shaking his head in a dazed fashion. 'Forgive me, Tammy,' he said at last. 'I've always known you were a beautiful woman, but tonight you're breathtaking!'

'Thank you.' He was exaggerating, and it was absurd to experience a deep thrill of pleasure spill through her veins like a warm caress at his compliment. Dagan had a reputation for being golden-tongued when the moment suited it, and instinct told Tamar he meant to amuse himself at her expense as the evening wore on. But she hadn't been immune to the deep warmth of his voice or the flash of desire in those deep blue eyes, and the knowledge of her weakness sent a shiver trembling through her.

'Cold?' Dagan had taken her coat from the wardrobe and held it out for her. 'Never mind, the car warms up very quickly. I've had it brought round to the front door for us, so there'll be no hanging around.'

Because she had no alternative, Tamar turned, sliding her arms into the silk lining of her smart black coat with its imitation lynx collar. Desperately aware of Dagan's nearness, the faint scent of aftershave, the warm skin smell of freshly showered male, she moved quickly away, hugging the coat around her and asking anxiously, 'Should we leave together? I mean, if people see me get into your car...' Her sentence trembled into silence as Dagan's mouth tightened ominously.

'What do you suggest, my dear Tammy? That I drive round to the back exit for you? Or pick you up further down the block? Or would you prefer to arrive at the restaurant by bus?' The asperity of his tone assaulted her. 'Or is this your way of saying you've had second thoughts and you don't intend to come with me after all, hmm?'

'I gave you my word and I've no intention of breaking it!' she said tersely, defending herself against his ill-humour. 'I was just a little concerned about what people might think. Surely the last thing you want is to have your name linked with a member of your staff...'

'That depends on which member,' he returned infuriatingly. 'It wouldn't be the first time, and it probably won't be the last. I can assure you I have little regard for my own reputation—and as for yours...'

'Yes?' Her eyes flashed grey fire, daring him to insult her.

'During all the time I've been here, I've never heard one word spoken to your detriment, not one boastful claim made regarding your favours, nothing but a respectful, rather envious curiosity about how you fill your spare time. Believe me, Tammy, you are regarded in INI with the same awe as that commanded by Calpurnia in ancient Rome.'

So she was like Caesar's wife was she—above suspicion? Good, that was precisely the image she had wished to project. As for her spare time, she hardly thought her curious colleagues would be interested to know it was chiefly spent reading, trying her hand at watercolours and visiting or entertaining some of the many friends she still had in the Westcliff area.

'I'm glad,' she said simply. 'It makes life much less complicated.'

'I'm glad too,' Dagan told her smoothly, placing a firm hand beneath her elbow and steering her towards the door. 'If only because as far as INI is concerned in this country at the moment *I* am Caesar!'

Biting her lip to hide her mixed chagrin and amusement, Tammy followed him into the executive lift. Dagan Carmichael was arrogant, autocratic and unbelievably egotistical. They were all attributes she hated in a man, and would go a long way to neutralising his charm, his charisma and his undeniable physical beauty.

CHAPTER SIX

THE RESTAURANT Dagan took her to was part of a country inn, set apart from the lounge bar by glass-panelled doors. Dark wood tables set in discreet alcoves gleamed with polish, the glasses sparkled beneath subdued warm pink lighting, and the spotless white napkins were a foil for the silver cutlery. Comfortable high-backed bench seats provided a luxurious resting place, causing Tamar to utter a sigh of pleasure as she sank down in their welcoming warmth.

'What a lovely place!' she said enthusiastically, her eyes drawn to the log fire burning in a traditional ingle-nook. 'It's authentic, isn't it?'

Dagan nodded. 'Of course, it's been renovated over the years, but it still has some of the original oak beams in the roof, and the food's first-class.' He handed her a menu. 'What will you have to drink?'

She chose a dry sherry to start with and a Riesling to complement the lobster she had selected as her main course, having paid Dagan the compliment of not allowing the price of the dish to influence her selection.

They ate their first course in silence, Dagan having chosen smoked salmon before steak *chasseur* and Tamar mushrooms *bourgignon* as a starter.

'Delicious!' she told him with a smile, placing her knife and fork down on her empty plate. 'I haven't eaten so well for years, barring Christmas dinner, of course!'

'Which you had in Bournemouth, if I remember correctly.'

'With my mother and sister Ruth, and Ruth's family,' she agreed, surprised when he pursued the matter.

'You've got nephews and nieces?'

'Nieces—Susan's six and Janet four. Ruth's six years my senior,' she explained, then added defensively, 'We had a marvellous time: a real old-fashioned Christmas— Christmas tree, decorations, carols round the piano with my brother-in-law Roger playing, Christmas stockings— the lot!'

'Very nice, too.' Dagan searched her face questioningly. 'Why do I get the feeling you expect me to decry it?'

Surprised he had read her so clearly, Tamar flushed slightly at her own gaucheness, irritated because she knew her translucent fair skin registered even the minutest change in the blood supply to it. Really, she should be able to hide her reactions better than that!

'It was hardly the kind of celebration a sophisticated businessman would enjoy,' she offered in explanation. 'But Ruth has always made a great fuss of Christmas, probably because as children ourselves we always missed having our father with us—'

'You were fatherless, then?' Dagan interrupted her explanation, a frown creasing his brow.

'Not until I was eleven.' Tamar made an empty gesture with one hand. 'But we might well have been for all we saw of Dad. He worked as an engineer on the oil rigs, and seemed to spend most of his life abroad. Facilities for wives and children were non-existent, so it was impossible for us to travel with him. When he did come home it was marvellous, but his visits were so few and far between, and his periods of leave never coincided with Christmas. Ruth and I both vowed that if ever we married and had children we'd wed a man whose job was local and we'd have a real family celebration every year...'

Dagan smiled at her enthusiasm. 'I take it Ruth didn't marry an oilman...'

'No, she didn't,' Tamar agreed, her own smile matching his. 'That was another oath we took—never to marry a man whose job took him away from his wife and family. Roger's in the teaching profession. He was deputy head at a school on the east coast until a couple of years ago, then he got the headship of a school in Bournemouth. It's marvellous, of course, because he has all the school holidays at home with the children.' She sighed with satisfaction. 'I feel good just being with them, you know. They're such a loving, tight-knit family, you feel they're impervious to harm from outside.'

'You sound envious,' Dagan remarked easily. 'And I had you all marked down as a career woman. Don't tell me you're the old-fashioned kind of girl, after all. One who would settle for the traditional ideals of marriage.'

Tammy paused for thought as the waiter presented her lobster with a side salad, nodding her thanks as he withdrew. She could bypass Dagan's question, but he was regarding her with the kind of concentration that demanded an answer, and why not tell him the truth? She wasn't ashamed of her own feelings.

'I believe in personal fulfilment,' she said carefully, 'and that's something that can't be laid down by a set of feminist rules, because it differs between individuals. To deny that fact by issuing a women's charter which doesn't take into account personal freedom is to deny the very liberation it claims to support.'

'Go on.' Ignoring his own meal, Dagan encouraged her, leaning forward, his dark blue eyes fixed on her animated face. 'So where do your own ambitions lie, Tammy?'

'I'm not sure yet,' she answered honestly. 'I've been raised in an era where domesticity is decried, yet I've never known anyone as happy as Ruth is, or less frustrated. She may be a full-time housewife, but her life isn't dominated by household chores. She's one of the most intelligent, vibrant, interesting women I've ever known, and she never complains about being bored. I honestly don't believe the days are long enough for her to fit in everything she wants to do.'

'Then marriage is your ideal?' he asked softly.

'Not necessarily.' Tamar picked thoughtfully at the lobster. 'It would depend on the circumstances. But then, neither is spending the rest of my days as a secretary. I enjoy working at INI, particularly since you came...' She stopped, trapped by her own words. So intent had she been on making her point, she had forgotten to be circumspect, and the gleam in Dagan's eyes showed he had appreciated her unwitting confession. 'What I mean is,' she corrected herself hurriedly, 'I enjoy the extra responsibility with which you've entrusted me, plus the increased sense of challenge in the atmosphere generally.'

'But,' he continued smoothly, 'I suspect you find little difference between catering for my needs and what would be the demands of an equally egocentric husband; except, of course, the latter would offer you more security.'

'They're your words, not mine!' She responded to his humour with an answering grin. A husband would, of course, offer her a lot more than security. He would offer her love and affection, a warm harbour in his arms each night, the opportunity of bearing his children, the joy of raising them to maturity, discerning in them as the years went by those same qualities that had made her fall in love with him. But she knew the ideal man would have to seek her out. It might be an old-fashioned belief, but husband-hunting was a hobby which held no appeal for her.

'Then why stay a secretary?' Across the table from her, Dagan had started on his own meal, pausing between mouthfuls to pose his question. 'Opportunities for women have never been better in the newspaper world. Have you ever considered selling advertising space? After all, you've all the facts and figures at your fingertips, plenty of contacts at the agencies—and a personal charisma that gives you a head start over your male rivals. In a couple of years' time you could aspire to head your own group, and from then onwards you could work your way up to senior management.'

'It sounds attractive.' Tamar leant forward eagerly, her imagination stimulated. 'But I'd need managerial support within the company to make such a change. The present policy is "horses for courses"!'

'That's where you're wrong, Tammy,' he corrected her gravely, limpid eyes surveying her challengingly. 'The present policy is whatever I decide it is. And if you want to change the course of your life, then I'll support your decision. Think about it.'

'I will. Thank you.' It was hardly what she had expected the evening to bring forth, and she wasn't sure whether she should feel dismayed or flattered. Was Dagan trying to get rid of her, or did he have a genuine admiration for her qualities? She bent her head, applying herself to the delicious dissection of the crustacean on her plate. There was no hurry to give him her answer.

Finishing profiteroles with an extra helping of cream topping them, she decided philosophically that she would have to go on a strict diet for the next two weeks. She hadn't weighed herself recently, but her mirror had told her the blue dress she was wearing outlined curves that little bit fuller than she would have liked. Like all sins, gluttony had a price to be paid, and one she would meet without flinching, ruthlessly cutting down on fats and sugar in the coming weeks until her outline dwindled to her satisfaction.

'I thought, if you've no objection, we'd finish the meal with coffee and brandy at my place.' Dagan's voice broke into her resolutions, continuing before she had a chance to raise objections, 'A brandy on top of the wine I've had tonight might just bring me over the top of the alcohol limit.'

Put like that, it was difficult for her to refuse, and why should she? Tamar fought down a slight feeling of unease. Her nervousness was probably due to the fact that as the non-driver she'd consumed more than half the bottle of wine during her meal. Dagan had been the perfect host—pleasant, attentive and not in the least flirtatious. The dinner was obviously his way of showing her he had accepted the regulations with which she controlled her life, she assured herself. What could be more pleasant than coffee and brandy, a continuance of their general conversation, perhaps even an update on Creta? Later, she could always get a taxi home. It was, after all, Friday night. No work for two days!

Dagan was watching her with one eyebrow tilted, as if he guessed the passage of her thoughts.

'Well?' he prompted gently. 'Do you have any objections, Tammy?'

'No, of course not,' she defended her decision stoutly. 'I'd be interested to see where you're living.'

The bungalow was more beautiful than she had imagined, she conceded a short while later, after he'd taken her on a conducted tour, before bringing her back to the main sitting-room.

'Adrian Conte's certainly done you proud!'

Dagan nodded. 'Nothing but the best for his executives while they're in favour.'

The hard edge of cynicism mocked his own position as he moved towards the banked-down fire, stooping to lift an air-vent and stepping quickly backwards as flames licked through the banked-up coal, sending dancing shadows round the softly lit room. No one would know better than Dagan that if one lived by the sword one died by the sword, Tamar realised, which might go a long way to explaining the thickness and brilliance of the armour he presented to the world.

'You must have a very efficient housekeeper,' she approved, turning her gaze from the fire towards where a flask of coffee, a decanter of brandy and two glasses stood ready prepared on a low table between two long leather couches.

'I'm surrounded by efficiency,' he agreed, coming towards her with a purposeful tread that had her rooted to the spot. 'But, desirable though it may be, *you* possess many more attributes than mere efficiency, my lovely Tammy.' He paused by the table to pour the coffee, and, lifting the decanter, filled the bowl of each glass.

A tremor of alarm vibrated down her spine. Oh, no, she should have listened to her innermost qualms instead of trying to rationalise them! The soft intimacy of Dagan's deep tones were much more daunting than the simple words he had spoken. What a fool she'd been to believe his interest in her had returned to being platonic! Men like him didn't know the meaning of the word! To them, seduction was a challenge, and resistance only heightened their pleasure in the chase.

'To us, Tammy!' Seemingly unaware of her disquiet, Dagan cupped the brandy glass in his strong palm for a few seconds before holding it out to her.

'Thank you.' She flashed him an insincere smile, moving away as she accepted the glass, speaking quickly in a voice that sounded too high-pitched to her own critical ears. 'It's been a very enjoyable evening, Dagan.' Rather than meet his eyes, she took a deep swallow of the spirit. It was smooth and powerful, rather like the man who had poured it, she thought a trifle hysterically, fighting an impulse to cough as the strong liquor burned her throat.

'Not ended yet, though.' Dagan took the glass from her hand, putting it with his own on the table while she watched him as if spellbound. 'Tammy,' he murmured, 'this pretence of yours has got to stop, you know. I'm a grown man who's long since tired of playing adolescent games of "touch me not".'

'It's not a game, Dagan.' She tried to justify herself, but it was impossible. She had never doubted Dagan's claim to adulthood! Everything about him shrieked of a brilliantly honed maturity, a male at the peak of his physical and mental capabilities. It was a heady scent of power and perfection that emanated from him, and she knew, to her detriment, she would never be entirely immune to it!

Now, as he drew her into his arms, she found she lacked the ability to oppose him. The evocative scent that surrounded her at that moment owed more to Dagan's physical presence than his mental prowess, she acknowledged weakly, the heady perfume of warm male skin, brandy, a trace of expensive cologne...

'Heaven alone knows how tested my will-power's been these last few hours,' he murmured, surveying her uplifted face through half-closed eyes. 'I've been wanting to kiss you from the moment you came out of my bathroom looking like a virgin about to be sacrificed to the Dragon!'

Tamar's lips, caught by surprise, parted in startled amusement at the imagery he conjured up, and lost the war before the first battle had been fought. Warm and demanding, Dagan's mouth sought and possessed her own, inflaming her senses with a mixture of tenderness and determination, totally undermining her resolve to stay calm and unresponsive.

His hands against her back gentled and caressed, increasing their pressure, supporting her spine so that she was drawn into such close contact with him, her breasts were crushed against his chest. She did what in moments of aberration she had dreamed of, raising her hands to his head, combing her fingers through the wealth of dark hair, pressing his head down in unconscious invitation to his mouth to continue with its ravishment of her senses.

She was gasping for breath when he released her, drawing her head down against his chest, still clasping her shoulders so that she couldn't escape from him even if she'd had the wish to do so.

Tamar's legs felt weak. Certain she would be unable to stand if she moved too quickly, she stayed where she was, feeling the thunder of Dagan's heart against her, its rhythm strong and heavy, quite unlike the erratic beating of her own pulse.

Her fingers clutching the smooth material of his jacket, she knew she should never have come. Despairingly she recognised and abhorred the wave of excitement that had made her lose control of herself beneath Dagan's assault. She had responded mindlessly to his physical presence, reacted to the powerful chemistry she had registered from their first meeting, in just the same way as she had fallen a slave to Martin Sanders. A shudder convulsed her. No way would she allow history to repeat itself! There might be a mutual attraction between Dagan and herself, but certainly no love.

'Come back by the fire...' Presumably he had mistaken her shudder of distaste for a cold shiver, she thought miserably as she allowed him to guide her towards one of the couches. Gathering all her strength, she refused to be seated, holding her hands out to the flames instead, and declining to meet his eyes, she forced a false brightness into her voice.

'I've been thinking, Dagan, if you don't feel up to driving I can always get a cab to take me home. It's not at all far from here.'

'And *I've* been thinking,' he returned smoothly, 'that as I don't feel at all like driving, you can spend the night here and I'll take you home tomorrow—or perhaps the day afterwards.'

'No!' The suggestion shattered her pose of sophistication as she jerked out her refusal, turning startled eyes to meet his quiet appraisal. 'As I said, it's been a pleasant evening, but I'm feeling a little tired. I really should be getting home.'

'What you feel, my darling, has nothing to do with tiredness.' Dagan ignored her pleading look. 'What you feel, as I'm sure you already know, is the kind of tension for which a very pleasant and effective cure exists.'

Tamar sucked in her breath, praying she could extricate herself without damaging anyone's pride. Dear heavens, she had to face this man across an office desk in a couple of days' time! While he was unlikely to deny her the right of choice, Dagan Carmichael wasn't the kind of man who was used to being refused, and might not take the experience kindly. She would not be the first secretary at INI to be summarily dismissed for the sin of saying 'no' to an over-amorous boss, nor the first to accept her fate without a fight, preferring not to court the embarrassment of alleging sexual harassment before a tribunal.

'Tammy—oh, Tammy, have you any idea of what you're doing to me?' It was almost a groan as he slid one arm around her waist, the other hand rising to cup her taut breast, its outline proudly visible through the soft dark wool of her dress. 'You're not going to deny you want me as much as I want you, are you?'

The agony of it was that she *did* want him! But he was barred to her. Even if he hadn't been who he was, she would never again allow herself to mistake physical arousement for a deeper emotion. That way lay disaster, not only for herself but for the unfortunate man whose chemistry played havoc with her own, and who was destined to remain unsatisfied. Damn Dagan for being the first man since Martin to have such a disastrous effect on her!

'Tammy?' His voice was suddenly uncertain. 'Tammy, what's the matter? You're not going to tell me that your adherence to old-fashioned customs extends to embrace unmarried chastity!'

'I don't have to explain my beliefs to you.' Incensed by the mocking incredulity she read on his handsome face, Tamar seized his hand, flinging it from her as she spun away from the enclosure of his arm, anger lending her resolution. 'Is staying the night with you an expected secretarial duty? Because if it is, then you should have told me at our first interview!'

The flash of anger that tautened his face was not unexpected, but Tammy had to exercise all her self-control not to flinch beneath it.

'Are you trying to tell me you were unresponsive in my arms a few minutes ago?' He caught her by the shoulder, his other hand lifting to touch the smooth glossiness of her fine hair with a caressing gesture, while his narrow-eyed gaze demanded an answer.

Tamar took a deep breath, striving to regain her composure, aiming to project herself as the cool sophisticate rather than the frightened virgin Dagan had scathingly hinted she might be. Probably he had no idea how near the truth his scornful surmise was, she determined grimly. Although *cautious* was a better word than *frightened*, in the circumstances!

'So I responded.' She shrugged graceful shoulders. 'You don't need me to tell you that you're an extremely attractive man.' She made herself meet his lowering gaze, ruthlessly quietening the warm surge of desire that uncurled deep inside her. 'You've wined me and dined me, and I was willing to show my appreciation to a degree, but I can't be bought for the price of a meal.'

In the silence that followed, Tamar heard only her own breath rasping in her throat and Dagan's laboured breathing, felt only the continued touch of his fingers against her hair, saw only the cool assessment in the depth of his cold stare, then he was moving away from her to toss down the contents of his own brandy glass, before turning on his heel to face her once more.

'I apologise for underestimating the value you place on yourself, Tammy, and stand suitably reproved.'

The coolness of his speech was reflected on his face as Tamar felt her heart sink. The last thing she had wanted was to alienate herself so thoroughly from him.

'Dagan, please,' she implored him a little unsteadily. 'I did tell you I never mix business with pleasure. I wouldn't have come back here with you if I'd thought...'

'I was only flesh and blood instead of a ruthless automaton?' A spark of antagonism glowed in the dark-lashed eyes as he interrupted her. 'I thought we'd been working closely enough together these last few months for you to have seen the man behind the manager!'

'I have,' she confessed, 'but it hasn't changed my beliefs.'

'Perhaps it's about time you started listening to your heart instead of your head, Tammy,' he suggested gently.

'Perhaps I will,' she riposted, quickly on the defensive, 'when my heart is involved!'

'Touché!' His mouth parted in a reluctantly admiring smile. 'Then I shall have to try to capture it, shan't I?'

Meeting his calculating stare, Tamar read with dismay that he saw her defiance as a challenge. For one brief moment she allowed herself to imagine him taking her by storm, sweeping away her protestations, plying her with words of loving entreaty. Then reality brought her to her senses.

Suppose she did let Dagan undermine her defences, how long would his interest in her last? Probably until his ego had been satisfied by her unconditional surrender—or until Adrian Conte moved him across the globe to another part of his empire—whichever came first. It was the first time she had admitted to herself that he was a formidable candidate to breach the barricades with which she had surrounded herself, and the knowledge filled her with foreboding.

'Don't look so concerned.' It was almost as if he'd read her thoughts. 'I don't intend to subject you to any sexual harassment. You're far too good a secretary to alienate in that way. I shall have to find some more subtle way of overcoming your resistance.'

'You'll be wasting your time, I'm afraid.' With a weary gesture she pushed her hair away from her forehead. The last thing she wanted to do was leave INI, but unless she could convince Dagan they had no future as lovers it would be impossible to stay there working for him.

'Time will be the proof of that, but the truth is, my dear Tammy, that you don't find me as repulsive as you'd like me to think,' he told her calmly.

Despite the warmth of the room, Tamar felt a shiver edge down her spine, as if she were being threatened. Dagan was a born fighter, achieving every goal on which he set his heart. It was clear that he wanted her, and his ego wouldn't allow him to consider the possibility of her not eventually submitting. The prospect was not reassuring!

'I've never found you repulsive,' she felt bound to reply, looking for some line of defence to substantiate her assumed lack of interest. 'But apart from anything else I'm personally involved with another man.'

'Neil Hathaway.' Dagan nodded perceptively. 'Yes, you demonstrated that fact very publicly, I seem to remember. Tell me, Tammy—did you spend your holiday in Greece with him last year?'

'With respect, that really is none of your business!' Her reply was haughty. How dearly she would have liked to lie, to pretend her relationship with Neil was an intimate one, and she was angry with herself for lacking the ability to do so.

'I thought not,' Dagan commented with infuriating smugness. 'I felt sure the office would have buzzed with that information if it had occurred!'

'As a matter of fact, he did ask me,' she told him coolly. 'But it just wasn't on. Quite apart from the fact that I couldn't arrange my holiday dates, I'd already agreed to spend the fortnight with an old schoolfriend of mine who's recently married a Greek. They have this marvellous villa on the coast not far from Athens.'

For a moment her face lost its tautness as her thoughts dwelled momentarily on Verona Constanidou and the idyllic life she was leading with her handsome husband Andreas who was obviously devoted to her and their baby son Alexos.

'And young Hathaway's attractions couldn't compete with the temptation of *ouzo* and *moussaka*?' Dagan's lips curled mockingly as he purred complacently, 'My dear Tammy, I do congratulate you. Your sense of priorities is unparalleled!'

His cool dismissal of the younger man brought a flush of colour to Tamar's face. Forced to take up the cudgels in Neil's defence, she riposted tartly, 'Neil is a good-looking, ambitious young man with a golden future ahead of him. He's both liked and respected in the business. In fact, he's considered one of the most eligible bachelors in advertising.'

'But not for you.' Dagan's reply smashed back instantly. 'You're no yuppie, Tammy, and the sooner you realise that, the better. Neil Hathaway can't give you anything you either need or want—believe me!'

Unfortunately, she did. It was a conclusion she had reached without Dagan's unwanted advice. Neil's philosophy on life tended to be shallow and changeable. She would no more trust her emotional well-being to him than she would to Dagan himself. However, that didn't stop him being an amusing and carefree companion whose company she would continue to enjoy when it suited them both.

It was not, however, something she intended to confide to Dagan. Consequently she kept her pretty mouth mutinously closed, holding her own counsel.

For a few seconds Dagan's thunderous gaze assessed her, only to be repulsed by her icy grey regard. Then he shrugged. 'Well, now we've settled that, I'll ring for a taxi for you, and while we're waiting for it to come I'll pour you another cup of coffee.'

Sitting in the taxi some twenty minutes later, Tamar stared miserably out of the window at the surrounding darkness. She had never expected to experience such violent reactions to Dagan Carmichael. His reputation had preceded him and prejudiced her against him, perhaps that was why she'd felt it unnecessary to erect additional barriers.

She just hadn't been prepared for the strength of her own responses. Even if it had been love she felt for him instead of mere physical attraction, there would have been no future in it, she thought morbidly. Dagan typified everything she hated in the male of the species—a man who had no roots and no allegiances. A drifter who took what he wanted where he found it and moved on to plunder fresh fields. An intruder whose coming was dreaded, whose presence was feared and respected and whose departure was eagerly awaited.

His self-control had been admirable, yet it had been terrifying too. She knew him well enough to realise that his withdrawal had been tactical rather than an accepted defeat. In the past he'd always got what he wanted. She would have to match his resolve if she were to best him.

Heaven knew, she was no prude, but she had a fierce pride that would always forbid her to be numbered among Dagan's conquests for the short time she would be in his orbit. If Neil Hathaway could offer her nothing, then Dagan Carmichael could offer her less than nothing!

CHAPTER SEVEN

DAGAN kept his promise. For the following two weeks he was the epitome of the perfect employer. Perfect as far as treating her in an impersonal and businesslike manner, that was, Tamar congratulated herself. If he hadn't continued to manifest the odd burst of ill-humour or impatience, she would have suspected he was sickening for something—or in love! Not that there was much chance of the latter, she told herself for the umpteenth time as she sat, pencil poised over her notebook, waiting for him to finish speaking on the phone. In the fast lane Dagan travelled the prevailing motto was 'bed them then shed them', and the evidence of his personal diary seemed to suggest that his previous girlfriends had reached the shedding stage.

How glad she was she'd made her stand when she had! So what if her heart did seem to beat a little faster in Dagan's presence, and when he smiled at her she felt intoxicated? It was a heady, exhilarating feeling—and she would enjoy it while she could. It couldn't last forever, and when Dagan left for fresh pastures at least she would be left with her dignity unimpaired.

'How are you fixed for overtime on Saturday night, Tammy?' His question took her by surprise, as he finished his call and replaced the receiver.

'Saturday's all right,' she agreed after a moment's pause. She'd already accepted a party invitation from Neil since having dinner with Dagan, but had reserved the coming Saturday for her own relaxation. 'What is it—an evening meeting?'

'In a way. I've invited the ad director of Creta Cosmetics and his wife to dinner at my place, and I need a hostess.'

'Oh!' For a moment she was taken aback. It didn't sound much like an overtime engagement, and what would she be expected to do? Did Dagan actually expect her to provide and cook a meal? It wouldn't be beyond her capabilities—but it was hardly within her accepted brief. A glance at his bland expression told her nothing.

'What exactly would it entail?' she asked carefully, determined not to commit herself too soon.

'Nothing beyond your talents,' he told her blithely. 'My housekeeper will get caterers in for the night, and apart from co-ordinating with them at the beginning, all you have to do is to look beautiful, act charmingly and enjoy the food. All of which I'm sure you'll do admirably.'

'But why me?' she protested weakly, not at all sure she wanted the role she was being offered. 'I'm no salesperson. Surely Fiamma . . .'

Dagan shook his dark head. 'Fiamma's played her part splendidly. Now I need your help. The one thing this dinner is *not* going to be is a sales session. It's purely social.' Pressing down the intercom button, he asked Pam in dulcet tones to bring in a tray of coffee, before walking across to the window to gaze silently down at the spread of the metropolis beneath him, leaving Tamar to sit in reluctant admiration of the tall, straight silhouette his back view presented to her.

She was on the horns of a dilemma, and already she knew that, though she might put up token resistance to his request, if he insisted she would accept it, even though she suspected it was a personal date masquerading as business. Her eyes lingered on the strength of his shoulders beneath the pale blue shirt which stretched across their breadth, taking a leisurely journey towards his taut waist before travelling in almost unknowing appreciation down the long legs in their silver-grey casing of wool and mohair.

The trouble with Dagan Carmichael was that, when he wanted to be, he was irresistible, as many women had found to their cost. An even greater problem was that he knew it and traded on it. Tamar sat more primly on her chair, stiffening her shoulders as she resolved never to let her own guard down where her attractive employer was concerned.

When Pam arrived with the silver tray with its matching coffee-pot, jug and sugar basin, which Dagan had provided for himself, together with the bone china cups which had been one of Tamar's first purchases for him, he returned to his desk to pour her a coffee just the way she liked it.

It wasn't unusual for Dagan to perform such a domestic duty. On occasions when both she and Pam were busy, he thought nothing of making the coffee himself and providing them both with cups. It might be dismissed as trivial by some people, but having worked for Hugh Drummond, who would have died of thirst rather than attempt to get his own refreshment, it was something that both she and Pam had chalked up in Dagan's favour.

Now she accepted his offering with a polite smile of thanks, as he explained how the final decision on whether the proposed media schedule for Creta Cosmetics as presented by the agency would be accepted would rest entirely with Leslie Frinton, the advertising director of Creta itself.

'He's sharp and he's been in the business a long time. He doesn't believe in keeping dogs and barking himself, which is why he uses an agency, but he's no yes-man, and he won't stand for someone trying to pull the wool over his eyes. We've made our presentation to him and told him quite honestly there's nothing to choose between the two contending media groups. He knows we've presented to the agency as well, and we've told him on the face of the evidence the latter should recommend he halve his budget between both groups to obtain maximum penetration plus frequency for his money.'

Tamar nodded, watching the lean, animated planes of Dagan's face, willing her mind not to remember how firm yet soft his mouth had felt against her own when he had kissed her. This was no time for vagrant thoughts, she reproved herself, leaning forward a little in her eagerness to hear the rest of his strategy.

'Naturally we didn't stoop to gossip-mongering about the intimate friendships of some of the principals. We kept our approach professional. Fiamma's been trained as an actress. She's adept at picking up cues, moulding her performance accordingly. Her brief was to play it by ear. Anyone could have delivered the facts and figures, but I asked Fiamma to do more than that. I wanted any-thing—anything at all that would keep us in there fighting.'

The light of battle darkened Dagan's eyes as Tamar nodded her understanding, wondering if she was doing him an injustice in thinking he wouldn't have been dis-appointed if Fiamma *had* used her seductive body to obtain preferential treatment for INI, if such a method would have worked. A trickle of apprehension travelled through her veins. Perhaps that had been his implicit intention.

'What she did discover,' he went on with every sign of satisfaction, 'was that Leslie Frinton is a rugby fan, and for the last month or so he'd been knocking himself sideways in an attempt to get tickets for the game at

Twickenham on Saturday. And we, of course, are in a position to play fairy godmother to him!'

'You mean he'd push half a million pounds of advertising budget our way in exchange for a ticket?' Tamar's incredulity was plain to see.

'Don't be so simplistic!' Dagan reproved her with a grin. 'Although love of sport and sex are probably the two great driving powers in many men, Leslie Frinton couldn't be bought that way. No, it simply means I've been given an opportunity to escort him to the match by courtesy of our sports department, and to entertain him and his wife afterwards in a friendly, informal setting with the prospect of establishing a strong enough rapport between us to make him query the omission of INI from the schedule when he sees it.' He leant back in his chair, long legs thrust out in front of him. 'That's the most we can hope for—and that's what we're going to try for! But not one word of selling. No mention of Creta unless he starts it, and then only polite response.'

Tammy stared down at her notepad. It sounded reasonable. She had worked in the mad world of advertising long enough not to be surprised at the seeming inconsequentials which determined the direction of huge sums of money. But why her and not Fiamma? Or, for that matter, since the dinner was to be purely social, why not one of Dagan's girlfriends? Surely one of them would have obliged?

She sent him a tentative look, not at all sure she wanted to accept. The memory of what had happened the last time she'd accepted his invitation was still too vivid to allow her to consider returning beneath his roof with equanimity. She was content with the status quo—why do anything to endanger it? On the other hand, to refuse would make her appear particularly uncooperative, especially since there was so much at stake for the company and him personally. The uncomfortable truth was that, if Hugh Drummond had ever made such a request to her, she wouldn't have thought twice about undertaking it.

'What's so difficult about making a decision, Tammy?' A devilish glint sparkled in Dagan's deep blue eyes as he fixed her with a brutal stare. 'Your precious virtue's not at stake. I'm only asking you to help entertain the guy—not go to bed with him!'

'Thank you for the reassurance!' His mockery stung her to the quick. Damn him for reading her thoughts, although it wasn't Leslie Frinton she had cast in the role of seducer. 'I imagine you would, though, if you thought it would work,' she snapped angrily.

Indolently, with no sense of haste, Dagan rose to his full height, walked towards her, took the pad from her hand and pulled her to her feet. Stiffening beneath his touch, Tamar pulled away from him, disturbed by the reaction her response had provoked. He let her go, standing facing her, hands rammed into trouser pockets, and glared down at her from his superior height, legs apart, his body tall and arrogantly poised.

'Then you suppose wrongly,' he said drily. 'You overrate your charms, my love.' She felt herself shrink as his insolent appraisal followed the lines of her body, a knowing little smile curving his mouth as if he were remembering when he had held her in his arms. 'In the first instance, if you want to sell your body for stakes as high as Creta, you would have to be an expert in the art of love.' His voice was quiet, but the words pierced her self-conceit with deadly accuracy. 'And I'm afraid you just don't qualify in that respect, do you?'

For a split second Tamar was stunned by the cruelty of his attack, her face draining of colour. Martin Sanders had said much the same thing to her, but on far greater evidence than Dagan. Had her kisses been so inexperienced, then? To her those shared moments of intimacy with Dagan had been breathtaking. Now he was belittling them and undermining the self-confidence she had striven so hard to resurrect after Martin's bitter attack.

'And in the second instance,' he was continuing evenly, his eyes narrowing slightly as he saw her colour recede, 'the only person I have in mind to share your bed in the near future is myself.'

Tamar swallowed convulsively as the soft, determined avowal of intention penetrated into her brain, trying to find something sophisticated and dismissive to say in reply and failing miserably. For two whole weeks she had been congratulating herself on having diagnosed Dagan's interest in her as ephemeral and having effectively nipped it in the bud. How wrong she had been! Beneath the façade of the chief executive, the dragon had only been lying dormant!

It was Dagan who broke the silence that quivered between them. 'Just your social graces, that's all I'm asking you for, Tammy. Your ability to converse, your smile, your charm. They have a value of their own, and one which I feel certain my guests will appreciate. As I said at the start, the underlying purpose of the dinner is business, and your attendance will be treated as overtime working on the company's behalf. You are, of course, at liberty to refuse without an explanation if you choose to do so. Well?'

Tamar steeled her shattered nerve, determined not to give him the satisfaction of seeing how much she'd been injured by his previous gibe, or flustered by his reference to sharing her bed. By putting the matter so clearly on a payment basis, he had effectively forced her hand. She made a gesture of indifference with both hands. 'Since you rate my social qualities so highly, then certainly I'll place them at the company's disposal.'

Without waiting for his reaction, she repossessed her notepad and forced her legs to carry her out of his office and away from his disturbing presence.

Tamar chose to wear a cream dress for the occasion. Tailored in the finest wool, its softness flattered her figure, its deep V-neckline balanced by long, close-fitting sleeves, the skirt sculpting the curve of her hips before flaring into fullness just below her knees. Regarding herself critically in the mirror, she knew she needed something to alleviate the classic plainness of the dress, something to rest on the pale skin displayed by the low-cut neck.

Almost reluctantly she took Dagan's Christmas gift from its box, appraising its delicate beauty. With a sigh of submission she placed it round her neck. Nestling in the hollow of her throat, it was the perfect accessory. Why not? She shrugged her shoulders at her reflection. Dagan had said it was for her past efficiency, not her future favours. If he read into it a message it didn't possess, then it would be her pleasure to disenchant him. Moving quickly, before she could change her mind, she selected a short scarlet woollen coat from her wardrobe, slipped her arms into its warm sleeves and phoned for a taxi.

Now, sitting at the oval rosewood dining-table, she felt able to relax. At the start of the evening she'd been tense and nervous, but the food and wine had been excellent, and she'd found both Frinton and his wife Margaret eminently likeable.

It was after the meal, while the caterers efficiently cleared the table, that Dagan, at Margaret's request, conducted his guests round the luxurious bungalow, obviously delighted when Leslie went into raptures over the games room with its full-sized snooker-table.

'Now, that's something I do covet,' the older man said, looking like a small boy confronted with a sack of Christmas toys.

'Do you fancy a game now?' Dagan raised an enquiring eyebrow. 'I'm sure the ladies will excuse us.'

Margaret's ready smile confirming the supposition, the two women left them setting the table up for a game, and returned to the warm comfort of the drawing-room with its soft leather couches and open fire.

'This really has been a lovely day.' Margaret curled up comfortably in the corner of one of the couches. 'Do you know, I thought at any moment we were going to have charts and computer print-outs thrust at us, and some heavy selling—that's what usually happens on these occasions. Frankly,' she said, casting a subtle smile at Tamar, 'it's only because Les was so desperate to go to Twickenham that he even considered Dagan's invitation.' Her hands reached towards the flickering blaze. 'This has been one of the least pressurised days he's had in ages, and I know he's appreciated every minute of it!' She let her eyes drift over the younger girl. 'Dagan Carmichael's not much like his public image, is he?'

'That depends,' Tamar responded cautiously, alerted to the older woman's deep curiosity. 'He's a very clever, dynamic, hard-working businessman.'

'And very good-looking and absolutely full of devastating charm.' Margaret shot her a sly glance. 'But there's no evidence on show tonight as to how he got the nickname of the Dragon Man.' Her pleasant face broke into a mischievous smile. 'Is he really as ruthless as he's painted—or am I to believe you've succeeded in taming him?'

'Me? Good heavens, no!' Tamar denied the supposition with alacrity, wishing to claim no hand in the moulding of Dagan's character. Her only attempt at bringing him into line had failed miserably, she reminded herself. 'Personally I've never found him ruthless.' It was her job to protect his image, she told herself firmly, nevertheless she was aware she was speaking the truth. 'His nickname's as much to do with his Welsh heritage, I imagine, as to his personality,' she improvised.

'Welsh?' Startled eyebrows rose above Margaret's wide eyes. 'I thought he was Canadian, although he's got no discernible accent.' She leaned forward eagerly. 'Tell me, does he speak Welsh?'

'I really don't know.' Tamar returned her gaze with interest. 'I've never asked him.'

'Well, well, that's something I'll have to find out before we leave.' Margaret laughed softly. 'It's almost a lifetime since I've heard my native tongue spoken.'

She shook her head wonderingly, while Tamar said a little uncomfortably, 'I shouldn't count on it. I understand it's a long time since Dagan left his homeland.'

'I don't think it's something you ever forget entirely.' Margaret stared at the fire. 'I keep promising myself to go back, but somehow I never do.'

With a little prompting she proved only too eager to talk about her homeland and the happy childhood she'd had there. Tamar listened with real interest, enjoying her companion's marvellous gift for story-telling, until the older woman broke into her own reminiscences with a start of alarm.

'Good heavens, is it so late already? I'm afraid we'll have to interrupt the snooker game, or Les will play all night, and we've got a long drive ahead of us.'

Cautiously Tamar led the way back to the games room, opening the door gently so as not to disturb the players. Clearly the frame was drawing to an end. Dagan was lying at full stretch down one side of the table, the toe of one long leg in contact with the floor, his chin practically balanced on the cue itself as he slanted his glance down its length.

His jacket had been abandoned, but his shirt-sleeves cuffed with gold were still in place. For a breathtaking moment Tamar gazed at the picture he made, glad no one else could see or translate the emotion on her face as her appraising glance travelled up the tensed muscle of calf and thigh, followed the lean, taut curve of his hips, dwelt on the slight movement of his shoulder as he judged his position on the cue ball. Helplessly she watched, as if mesmerised. It was poetry in motion, and she wished she could stand there enjoying the sight of him forever.

Smoothly the cue ball struck the last black to send it safely into the bottom pocket, and Dagan straightened his long length from the table as Margaret spoke softly in a language Tammy had never heard before.

Listening to Dagan's surprised laugh, she saw real pleasure on his face, then he and Margaret were conversing in a tongue both guttural and mellifluent.

Leslie laid down his cue resignedly. 'I'm afraid Dagan has the edge over me in height and reach,' he told Tamar with a wry grin. 'Quite apart from the fact that he's a considerably better player!'

'Does that mean you lost?' Tamar asked sympathetically, wondering how politic it had been for Dagan to beat the man when he wanted his business!

'I fancy our Mr Carmichael wins most things he plays for!' Leslie shot a look of assumed annoyance in Dagan's direction. 'Now it turns out he's from the valleys, too.

I shan't hear the last of this night for a long time, I can tell you!' But his glance at his wife was full of affection and amusement.

They both left shortly afterwards, at the last moment Margaret turning to Dagan and speaking to him earnestly in Welsh. From the glances she kept throwing towards Tamar, it seemed the latter was the subject of the conversation. Uneasily Tamar wondered what Dagan found so amusing about what was being said, as they both smiled like conspirators.

'That was a splendid afternoon and evening!'

Dagan threw himself down on one of the couches, beckoning Tamar to join him, as the sound of a car engine announced that their guests were on their way.

'Come and sit down for ten minutes, Tammy, then I'll drive you home.'

For a second she hesitated before deciding not to provoke him by refusing, then thankfully she sank down beside him, only now realising how tired she felt. Arriving by taxi at the bungalow in ample time to supervise the caterers as arranged with Dagan, before he and his guests returned from the match, hadn't been hard work, but she had been apprehensive and only realised how much now the ordeal was behind her.

'They're a very nice couple,' she remarked contentedly, deliberately keeping space between herself and the man stretched out beside her.

'Aren't they?' Ignoring her boundaries, Dagan slid one arm round her shoulders in a brotherly fashion, his hand touching her sleek blonde hair as it caressed the shoulders of her pale cream dress. 'It was a very successful venture, and you were superb, Tammy—just perfect. If Les Frinton isn't aware of our existence now—he never will be.'

'Thank you,' The touch of his hand on her hair was disturbing, and she prayed he wouldn't guess how fast her heart was beating. Ten minutes, he had said. Surely she could keep her equilibrium for so short a period?

'How strange that Margaret should be Welsh, and that both of you should speak the language.' She kept her voice lightly conversational, as Dagan's fingers caressed the sensitive skin at the nape of her neck, steeling herself not to show any reaction.

'It was the only language I spoke until I was six.' He settled more comfortably, and she felt with a quiver of excitement the length of his thigh fleetingly touch her own. 'Until I was sixteen I was bilingual, after that...' he shrugged broad shoulders, 'it was more important to conform, and that meant English only, but I've never forgotten it—although I imagine my accent's pretty grim!'

Looking at the strong line of the profile just inches from her own face, Tamar thought what a long way he'd travelled from the valleys of his native land in a comparatively short time. Did he regret his absence as much as Margaret had confessed she regretted hers?

As if he guessed her thoughts, Dagan gave an odd little smile. 'At sixteen I had to make the most important decision of my life—to go down the pit or leave Wales, because in the village where I lived there was no other choice if you wanted to put food in your mouth.'

'How about your parents?' Tammy ventured, fascinated by this glimpse into his youth, and fractionally forgetting she hadn't intended to prolong their time alone together. 'Did they pressurise you at all?'

Dagan's lips twisted ruefully. 'I'm afraid my mother had left my father a long time before then. She couldn't cope with the life of a miner's wife. She was a city girl, you see, wanting the bright lights and the music.' He stared into the fire, as Tamar experienced an unexpected surge of compassion for him. Suddenly he was vulnerable. It was a quality she'd never associated with him, and the unexpected realisation ran like an electric shock through her system.

'I never blamed her,' he continued softly. 'From what I remember of her she was very beautiful. She deserved something better than what my father could give her.' His strong, soothing fingers moved from Tamar's neck to trace the line of her shoulder, and still she made no move to shrug it away. 'Love, after all, is a fleeting pleasure at the best of times,' he said reflectively. 'And at the worst of times a non-existent one!'

'And you called me a cynic,' she reminded him softly. 'Tell me more about your father, Dagan.'

'A realist, not a cynic, Tammy,' he corrected her gravely before replying to her request. 'My father died shortly after my fourteenth birthday—some pit-related disease of the lungs.'

'I'm sorry.' The words seemed so inadequate, yet they came from her heart. She too had lost her father at an early age, but she'd had her mother and sister. Dagan had hardly enjoyed a promising start to his life, yet he had achieved so much! Intrigued, she waited for him to continue.

'I was living with my uncle.' He closed his eyes, his deep voice steady and emotionless. 'All my cousins went down the mine, and it was expected of me as well, but I shook them all by joining the Merchant Navy. I served my contract, saved most of my money and left the ship in Canada. Work was difficult to find, and I did many things before getting a job as a warehouseman in a large newsagent's. One of the circulation reps of a local paper befriended me and put a word in on my behalf when a vacancy arose in his department.' He stirred, opening his eyes to slant her a smile. 'When Adrian Conte took the group over, he asked me why he should continue to employ me.' The smile turned into a grin that made Tamar's unprepared heart flip over like a pancake on Shrove Tuesday. 'He must have liked my answer, because he took me under his wing—and I think the rest of the story's pretty well-documented!'

Tamar nodded, finding it difficult to believe the celebrated Dagan Carmichael, beloved of the media gossip columns, was sitting here beside her, not a demigod as so often portrayed, but warm flesh and blood, much more man than machine! With an effort she forced her mind away from the quality of his maleness, finding it too disturbing. Dragging her attention back to what he had said, she nodded.

'Yes, from the rags of a small-town local paper to the riches of a multi-million newspaper empire!' Her soft mouth lifted at the corners as she held her head questioningly a little to one side. 'Do you ever long for your lost green valleys, I wonder—or are you happy with the bright lights you chose?'

He turned the full battery of his dark blue gaze on her questioning face, and if she hadn't know better she could have imagined her simple enquiry had hurt him.

'You make me sound very mercenary, my lovely Tammy.' The dark silk tones accused her. 'Yes, I do sometimes long for the valleys and mountains and waterfalls I knew so fleetingly. But bright lights? No. All I ever wanted to do was to be able to feel the sun and wind and rain on my face, to stretch my limbs and move on the face of the earth like a man: not to be cramped and confined like a mole underground. It wasn't the bright lights I chose, Tammy—just the sunlight.'

A feeling of shame overcame Tammy at the obvious sincerity of his reply. She hadn't expected such a confession from the man at her side, and now she regretted her question. Suddenly she understood his need to take the exercise another man in his position would have abhorred: his tendency to walk around London rather than use his company car for short journeys and the daily trek up the stairs to his office confirmed what he had just told her. Knowing what he'd escaped, no wonder he took every opportunity to stretch his limbs and move like a man!

Her heart was actually aching with compassion for the young man he'd been as his hand left her shoulder to drift casually down her arm in an action that was no longer brotherly.

'And like most things I set my mind on, I obtained it,' he murmured as his fingers moved in open caresses on the firm flesh of her upper arm, before sliding off to continue their soft, stroking movements against the side of her breast. 'Success doesn't always come easily, but I have two attributes that give me a head start—constancy of purpose and staying-power. So why don't you stop fighting me, Tammy? It's a battle you're going to lose sooner or later, and in the meantime you're wasting a lot of precious time for both of us.' The devastating blue eyes smiled at her from behind their dramatic shield of dark lashes.

CHAPTER EIGHT

MOMENTARILY lost for words, Tamar knew she should get up, do anything to get away from Dagan's powerful presence, because he wasn't actually confining her to his side. Oddly her limbs seemed to be both burning and frozen as she made herself meet the mesmeric eyes that looked so arrogantly at her.

It was as if her mind had split into two parts, one warning her of untold dangers in remaining a moment longer, the other prompting her to register how vitally aware of his body heat she was as it reached through the fine cotton shirt he wore. Vagrant, uncontrollable impulses took over control of her rational thought processes. She was experiencing a powerful need to touch him, to feel for herself the strength and resilience of those muscles she had seen so elegantly displayed across the snooker-table.

He was as potent as a drug, a narcotic which unwitting victims thought they could handle and then found to their horror that they were plunged into a nightmare world where they lost control over their own actions. That was how Dagan was affecting her. One taste, one touch and she was lost! How could she ever have thought she could spend even ten minutes alone in his company without responding to his arrant masculinity?

'Stop punishing both of us, Tammy. You know as well as I do that it's inevitable, you and I.' His strong fingers touched the gold at her throat. 'That's why you wore my brooch, isn't it, my love? To give me the pleasure of taking it off when the time comes?'

'You said there were no strings attached to it,' she protested furiously, fighting the warm surge of desire his words had engendered, and trying to contain it.

'Neither were there.' His dark lashes brushed his cheeks as his eyes narrowed. 'But *you* never believed that, did you, Tammy? So when you wore it tonight you were telling me something.'

'No... I...' She tried to get to her feet, but the weight of Dagan's hand on her shoulder detained her.

'Heaven help me, Tammy, I've never forced myself on an unwilling woman or pursued a lost cause! But whatever it is that's keeping you out of my arms has nothing to do with what you feel for me. Even Margaret Frinton could see that!'

So that was what they had been laughing about together! Tamar flushed with angry embarrassment, furious with herself for displaying to others what she wouldn't even admit to herself.

'So you know my feelings better than I do?' she asked sarcastically, grey eyes blazing at his dark face.

'I know you very well,' he countered softly. 'After all the hours we've spent in each other's company, we're hardly strangers, are we? I wouldn't claim to read you as an open book, my sweet, but there are some things you can't hide from me, and at this moment your anger would seem to prove me right. For pity's sake, Tammy, I never thought you'd let your principles blind you to what's happened!'

An element in his husky voice warned her that if she was to leave without incident she must arouse her lethargic limbs and do so immediately, but before she could gather her senses together Dagan had captured her mouth with his own, the cry of surprise in her throat stifled as the tide of sensuality rising within her refused to remain in check a moment longer.

Once during the evening, flushed with wine and liqueurs, she had fantasised about what it would be like to be Dagan's wife, to stand beside him while their guests left and then, afterwards, in front of the flickering flames, to be taken in his arms... Ruthlessly she had banished the thought from her mind, but it had been the moment she should have realised the truth. She was in love with him! Having set her mind against everything she believed him to be, she knew her heart had betrayed her.

He was right—they were no longer strangers. She had shared a vital part of his life for nearly four months. She had experienced his warmth and vitality at close hand, his drive and compassion. She knew his humour and understood his goals. She was aware of his taste in food and wine, his politics and his beliefs, and, heaven help her, his desires! Working with him she had learned more about his personality and character in that time than she could have ever done if their meetings had been limited to social dates. And this was the net result—she loved him!

Now fantasy and reality were merging into one beneath the practised expertise of his kiss, and she was loving every minute of it. Sensitive and soft, his lips explored her soft, trembling mouth, sending painful tremors of longing surging through her. Smoothing her hair back from her face, Dagan touched her forehead, her nose, her cheeks with delicate, searching caresses, soft and exciting. And all the time she could feel the tension mounting inside him, the powerful hunger gathering behind the gentle façade he was presenting.

Hearing his breathing become heavier and faster, feeling his hands roaming convulsively over her upper body, Tamar knew she was flirting with a highly potent danger, yet was powerless to call a halt to it as her eager flesh clamoured for more.

Her dazed mind was still trying to cope with the revelation that it was more than just physical attraction that made her so compliant in his arms when his fingers discovered and lowered the long zip fastener at the back of her dress. She made an automatic gesture of negation, moving her hands to her own shoulders in an effort to prevent him from pushing the material away.

'Let me see you, Tammy.' It was a thick command. 'I've waited so long to enjoy this moment. If you've any pity, don't deprive me now!'

Pity had nothing to do with her obedience. Moved by the powerful intensity of his plea, she didn't hesitate. Women sunbathed nearly nude all over the place now. Why should this be any different? But it *was* different, and they both knew it as Dagan, reading the compliance in her luminous grey eyes, brushed aside her unresisting hands, easing the dress down to reveal the cream lace bra that cradled the aching burden of her breasts.

This time she made no attempt to stop him, entranced by the seriousness of his tense face, the glimpse of his tongue behind parted lips as his strong, deft fingers smoothed the delicate, fragile little straps away from her shoulders.

How strange, she thought, that his capable, large masculine hand with its long fingers and blunt nails could be so gentle as it cupped her pale flesh. How odd that the strong mouth that could snarl orders and snap commands could turn into a soft, seeking creature that wanted only to devour and succour.

As a warm tide of fervour built to a flood in her untutored body, Tamar offered no resistance to the teasing, darting pleasure Dagan's tongue took from her, surrendering her body with little moans of delight, aware that the warmth of the fire was nothing compared to the burning flames that were searing through her cells, encouraged and nourished by Dagan's tenderness and passion, exorcising for all time the scars left by her first encounter with an aroused male.

Instinctively she knew this was how it should be. Knew she had to touch Dagan in return: to discover his naked skin as he was learning hers. With shaking fingers she undid the buttons of his shirt with surprising ease, encouraged by his soft grunts of approval, and slid her hands over the heated flesh beneath to discover the heavy pounding of his heart beneath her palm.

Her soft, curious fingers teased his skin, discovering the secrets of muscle and sinew. Eyes closed, remembering the first time she had seen him half stripped, she explored the subtle difference of structure between male and female, her breath coming light and fast as his lips paid homage to her tender flesh.

'Come here, sweetheart,' Dagan muttered, half lifting her, half carrying her to the floor and curling himself round her as she subsided on the deep-piled rug before the fire.

Her body melting, throbbing with a desire she had never experienced before, Tamar lifted her arms to draw him down to her, desperate to feel his weight commanding her, as if that alone could quell the trembling tumult that threatened to make her whole being dissolve.

Locked in his arms, feeling the hard male contours of his body seeking refuge in her woman's shape, she knew the need to submit to him was overwhelming and irrefutable.

'Let me love you, darling.' His voice was a broken murmur against her breast. 'Let me love you and teach you how to love me. Stay with me tonight, Tammy. I want to bury myself in your softness and sweetness. I want to wake up in the morning and find your face on the pillow beside me. Let me love you, Tammy.'

'Dagan...' Her voice shook and she inhaled a deep breath, trying to steady it. 'Yes' was such a silly, simple little word to say in the circumstances when in saying it she was giving him much more than her permission to take her body and make it his own: when she was giving him her heart and her love for as long as he wanted it.

'Trust me, sweetheart.' Even while she fought to form the basic word of willingness, his lips were seeking hers, erotically persuasive as his tongue spoke its own message of seduction, making her body shudder in a spasm of interwoven pleasure and pain. 'I swear you'll be safe in my care. Do you think I'd let anyone or anything hurt you, least of all myself?'

Smiling mistily at his intense face as he finally released her, Tamar, on the point of giving him the answer he was pleading for, hesitated as she detected the sound of a car approaching. The bungalow was far enough off the beaten track for any traffic to be making directly for it.

'Dagan, listen.' She pushed herself upright, arranging her clothing to cover her nakedness. 'Someone's coming!'

'Must have taken a wrong turning,' he said, brushing her protest aside. 'If anyone knocks here, we won't answer the door.'

'But it may be Les and Margaret,' she insisted, as the car braked outside. 'Perhaps they've had an accident or something.'

'Damn!' Reluctantly he rose to his feet, buttoning his shirt and tucking it smoothly inside his belt, a frown creasing his brow, as the sound of a car door being firmly closed echoed round the room. 'Look, whoever it is, I'll get rid of them as quickly as possible.' His mouth twisted wryly. 'Don't go anywhere without me, Tammy!'

As he went out of the room, Tammy quickly pulled her dress into position and re-zipped it. Using her fingers, she pushed her hair back into what she hoped was an acceptable style. There wouldn't be time to re-do her make-up as she heard light footsteps on the path outside. She would just have to hope it was a false alarm, or Dagan's late visitor would be content to sit in the dimly lit room as it was.

Painfully aware of her swollen breasts and the hollow ache in her loins, she prayed their visitor wouldn't stay long. Her ears keyed to the front door, surprisingly she fancied she heard the sound of a key in the lock, followed by Dagan's exclamation of surprise, then a woman's laugh. If she'd had any sense she would have stayed where she was, but her intelligence seemed to have disappeared together with her caution as a tight constricting pain which could only be jealousy scythed through her.

Without a second thought, she moved swiftly to the door and flung it open.

The woman in Dagan's arms was one of the most beautiful Tamar had ever seen. A classic beauty, but not cool: an indefinable gleam sparkling in violet-blue eyes, a small, perfect nose, and a mouth as soft and dewy as a lipstick advertisement, her loveliness was breathtaking. Straight ash-blonde hair curved in a fringe across a smooth forehead and fell to just beneath her ears. She was dressed in a deep blue velvet leisure suit which showed to advantage her high, round bust, tiny waist and shapely bottom above long, elegant legs. With her black patent high-heeled shoes she must have been about five feet nine, because she fitted against Dagan's lean body as if she had been made for it. She was expensive and cherished and obviously welcome, as she shot Dagan a wicked, laughing look from beneath curling lashes.

'Surprised, darling?' She ran pink-tipped nails through his dark hair, obviously enjoying his discomfited reaction. 'I'm sorry I couldn't give you notice of the change of day, but in the end it was touch and go whether I made it or not. Still,' she looked around the pleasant hall, obviously very much at home, 'now I am here, I'll get you to take my luggage out of the car.'

To do Dagan justice, he looked dumbfounded, shaken and dazed with shock. If she hadn't been so utterly devastated herself, Tamar would have laughed. It was like a French farce. Just when the hero was ready to seduce the new woman in his life, an old flame appeared. For one thing was clear—whoever this woman was, she was no stranger to either Dagan or his home.

As if realising for the first time that he wasn't alone, the blonde unfastened herself from his neck and turned with a pleasant smile to Tammy.

'Please forgive me,' she said politely. 'Dagan and I are very old *friends*.' She gave him a sliding glance of amusement as she emphasised the word. 'You can see he wasn't expecting me just now. I've quite taken his breath away—or he'd introduce us.'

'Yes, forgive me, Carrie. Your arrival tonight was certainly—unexpected.' Dagan was recovering fast. 'Carrie, this is my secretary, Tamar Phillipson. She's been helping me entertain some clients who've just left.' His steady gaze encompassed Tamar. 'Tammy, this is Carrie Denvers.'

Tammy took the readily extended hand, exchanging a brief, firm handshake, before the other woman turned briskly towards the sitting-room.

'Come and join us, won't you, Miss Phillipson?' she invited smoothly. 'Or were you just about to leave?'

It was as polite a dismissal as Tamar had ever been given. In the circumstances she welcomed it. She felt sick. Carrie was no casual girlfriend: she had a key to the house, acted as if she had every right to be there, assuming the role of its mistress, and from Dagan's acceptance of her behaviour it seemed he had no objection to that.

If Carrie's arrival had been delayed by another minute—even another second—she, Tamar, would have spilled out her confession of love to Dagan. As it was, she had been spared that humiliation. She was no naïve fool to imagine Dagan's interest in her promised any kind of long-term commitment, but she had hoped he'd respected her enough to ensure that his life was free of other emotional complications before offering her a relationship. A relationship! She gritted her teeth in an effort to keep her face politely composed. Perhaps she was a naïve fool, after all! Everything that had happened showed that all Dagan had been interested in was a one-night stand. Instead of hating the other woman, she should be feeling gratitude towards her for arriving when she had and stopping her making a terrible mistake.

'Mr Carmichael was just going to phone for a taxi for me when we heard your car draw up,' she said coolly, proud of her ability to speak in a voice that didn't match the trembling of her limbs.

'Look, Tammy—' Dagan glanced uneasily from her towards Carrie, who was regarding them both with open curiosity.

'I really do have to get back.' Her eyes dared him to prolong her agony, accusing him of unmentionable sins in their sparkling animosity.

With a shrug of his shoulders he walked to the phone and dialled a number.

The moments of waiting seemed endless, as she sat on the edge of one of the couches. She supposed she joined in some of the general conversation, but afterwards she could remember nothing of it, only the dreadful, empty ache that had grown into a deep physical pain deep down inside her.

When Dagan took her outside and thrust an arm round her shoulders, she bore his touch with stoical indifference.

'Tammy!' There was a pressing urgency in his voice. 'I can explain about Carrie.'

In the darkness his eyes were troubled midnight pools.

'I'm sure you can,' she said wearily. 'But please don't trouble on my account.' She hadn't expected a lot from Dagan—only that he should have finished one affair before embarking on the next. 'It was very interesting meeting her. I hope you both have a pleasant evening.'

At least he had the good taste not to attempt to kiss her as she swung away from his hold and opened the door of the waiting cab, climbing in thankfully, resolutely turning her head away from him as the vehicle drew away.

Reaching the sanctuary of her apartment, she stared at her pale face in the mirror, half expecting to see that she'd aged in years as well as experience. Her oval-shaped face and regular features were certainly no match for the exquisite Carrie, she registered bitterly. She must have been mad to fall for Dagan's honeyed words, when all he'd wanted was a female body to relieve the tension of separation from his regular mistress, for all her senses relayed the truth of Carrie's role in his life, even the slight trace of Canadian accent, which only now she recalled.

Her jaundiced eye caught the gleam of gold at her throat. With a small cry of disgust she tore it from her neck, snapping the slender chain as she did so, and flung it disdainfully into the back of the drawer.

Having spent the remaining hours of the night tossing and turning between short periods of light sleep, she was up early the following morning, determining to spring-clean her apartment in an attempt to purge her trauma in physical activity. Dressed in an old pair of jeans and a soft pink angora sweater that had seen better days, she systematically worked her way around each room, re-gardless of whether such Draconian measures were required or not.

Of course she would have to resign. No way could she go on working for Dagan, seeing him every day, sharing his confidences, watching his triumphs, desiring him with every fibre of her body while her heart was so bruised.

Logically, she couldn't even blame him. He had made no deliberate attempt to deceive her. Who better than herself to know the prevailing atmosphere in the media world was to live for the day? They were creative people, working hard and playing hard. To be honest, it was the element of excitement that had attracted her to the job in the first place.

She hadn't been able to see herself in a bank or in-surance company. Not for her routine. She had wanted the stimulus of deadlines, the thrill of belonging to a dynamic organisation whose lifeblood was the adver-tising revenue they could attract. It was a vicious circle. The more advertising INI got, the bigger papers they could produce, and the bigger papers attracted more readers, who in their turn attracted the advertisers.

She'd enjoyed being a part of that heady atmosphere of achievement; but after that initial painful branding as a teenager, she'd known her tranquillity rested in keeping emotionally detached from her colleagues.

Ruthlessly she picked up a pile of magazines and discarded them in the waste-paper basket. Now she had fallen into the trap she'd seen ensnare so many other girls. The only way left to escape was to get out!

Tomorrow she would give Dagan her contractual one month's notice. At least, she comforted herself, she wouldn't become the topic of conversation in the local pubs, as so many of her ex-colleagues had. She hadn't worked with Dagan so long not to know that he was neither retributive nor a man who would publicly discuss his private life.

By eleven she had done enough to satisfy her own exemplary standards. Stowing away the vacuum cleaner and putting the dusters into a bowl of hot water to soak, she ran herself a bath.

It wasn't that she was a prude, she told herself, relaxing in the perfumed water. She would never censure other people's behaviour, provided it was mutually enjoyed. It was just that she wasn't the type of woman who could carry on more than one affair at a time, or become involved with a man who could. Neither could she give herself to a man whom she didn't love. It was just her misfortune that she had fallen in love with Dagan Carmichael.

Stepping from the bath, she towelled herself vigorously, dressed in clean undies, and was about to choose a dress from the wardrobe when her bell rang.

Damn! she muttered to herself. Probably a Jehovah's Witness, and she was in no mood to be converted. Perhaps whoever it was would go away. The bell rang again, hard and long. Persistent! Tamar grabbed at her fleecy turquoise housecoat, buttoning it with hurried fingers before approaching the window and looking out into the street.

Dagan's Rover stood outside in the road. She had hardly got over the shock when the bell rang again—and again—and again.

If she resisted its urgent summons, perhaps he would go away. She was still hovering by the window when he came into view, walking down the path, but before she could draw a sigh of relief he turned and looked straight up at the window from which she was gazing. Quickly she retreated, but the renewed summons of the doorbell told her he had glimpsed her presence.

She had hardly expected him to come to her home. Yet now might be a better opportunity to tell him of her decision rather than in the office with the likelihood of constant interruption—provided he didn't come upstairs, of course. The bell rang again, summoning her urgently, denying her the opportunity to brush her hair and put on her make-up. At a time when she most wanted to be cool and positive, she was going to have to face Dagan looking like an *ingénue*.

Tying her belt tightly, she ran barefoot down the stairs, combing her fingers through her damp hair.

'I got you out of bed!' It was a flat statement as his brilliant blue eyes raked over her. 'I'm sorry, Tammy. I could have come back later if I'd known. The fact is, I thought you might not want to see me.'

She swallowed hard, not troubling to deny his supposition. 'Is something wrong at INI?'

It wasn't a silly question. The editorial staff were in on Sunday, and it wouldn't be the first time she had been asked to put in an appearance in an emergency.

'No.' His curt reply was dismissive. 'May I come in, please, Tammy?'

She stood back, allowing his access to the small square entrance hall. 'I'm sorry I can't invite you upstairs—I'm not alone.' It was the first time she had lied to him, although not the first she'd told lies on his behalf. A small, humourless smile curved her lips at the memory.

In a thick sweater which complemented the width of his shoulders and tough denims moulded to his long, muscled thighs, he looked a formidable opponent, all the more so now as his eyes narrowed to points of Prussian blue steel, piercing through the flimsy barrier of indifference she had erected against him.

'Hathaway?' he demanded peremptorily.

Fighting against the rapid pounding of her heart and the tremors which teased her spine, Tamar refused him an answer, contenting herself with holding her head a little higher and meeting his challenge without lowering her eyes.

'Yes, you're quite right. What you do in your own time is no concern of mine.' His smouldering gaze swept in a comprehensive assessment of her begowned figure as she felt heat stain her cheeks. 'But I owe you an explanation about Carrie——' he began.

'You owe me nothing, Dagan!' Tamar interrupted him as a bitter, galling pain ran through her like a lightning strike. 'For heaven's sake, I've never been under any illusion about the kind of life you lead!' She stiffened and pulled away from him as he took a step towards her.

'The kind of life you nearly became an integral part of yesterday,' he told her harshly.

'An occurrence I would have regretted deeply when I sobered up this morning!' she flung back. 'You can't imagine how grateful I am that Carrie returned to the love-nest when she did. Now, if that's all you came to say...' She hesitated delicately, sending a meaningful glance towards the stairs.

'Are you trying to tell me that the only reason you were prepared to make love with me was that you were drunk?' he asked disbelievingly. His keen eyes burnt into her, and she felt as if she were being branded. She mustn't let him see the effect he had on her, how his nearness sapped her strength, how easily she would fall into his arms if he opened them to her.

Tamar forced herself to speak coolly. 'I don't drink much as a rule. Yesterday I had a sherry before lunch, two or three glasses of white wine with the meal and a Benedictine afterwards. I was confused.'

'The hell you were!' Her shoulders were seized in a remorseless grip. 'The next thing you'll be telling me is that you don't remember what happened. That you don't know we were almost lovers!' His breath rasped as he pulled away to stare into her flushed face.

'I do remember that, to my shame.' For a few seconds she closed her eyes, blotting out the image of his furious face. 'It's something I never wanted to happen. I've told you how I feel about office affairs—they always end in disaster.'

'Some do, I grant you.' He brushed aside her quiet retort. 'But you can't generalise, Tammy. It's not un-known for some people to meet at work, fall in love, marry and live happily ever after. You can't turn your back on what we feel for each other for no better reason than that one of your friends had a bad experience.'

What we feel for each other... That was a laugh! What Dagan felt for her and what she felt for Dagan were different sides of different coins. What did he expect her to do? Wait until the ubiquitous Carrie disappeared again and take over from her? She drew in a deep breath, knowing the time had come to get it over with.

'Dagan, there's nothing more to be said. I don't play in the same league as you do, and I don't want to join. Now you're here, I might as well tell you—I've decided to leave INI. I'll let you have my official notice in writing first thing tomorrow.'

'You're being absurd, Tammy.' He stared at her, his dark brows drawn into a straight line across his forehead. 'You can't give up a job you love just because...'

'I can't work with you any more, Dagan! Isn't that a good enough reason?' she thrust back angrily. 'I don't *want* to work with you! Can't you understand that? I can't concentrate in an atmosphere of...' She choked into silence, unable to find a word to describe the heady, unsettling ambience that surrounded her in Dagan's presence.

He uttered a smothered oath. 'I can't let you leave because of me. Look, Tammy, if Carrie's the problem, then I swear to you she means nothing to me. The truth is...'

'Keep your truth, Dagan!' She raised her hands to shake his hold from her shoulders. The only thing his bad-mouthing of Carrie would do would be to lower her respect for him even further. 'Carrie—who she is or what she does—has nothing to do with my decision. I just feel I can't work with you.' Her throat was dry and burning, and she swallowed awkwardly to clear it. 'I can't give you the wholehearted allegiance you demand from your staff any more. Call it a clash of personalities, if you like, but by your own definition I feel there's no longer a place for me in your office.'

'I see.' The grimness of his tone told her she had won her point. 'Then if that's how you really feel about it— there's nothing I can do to persuade you to change your mind?'

'Nothing,' she whispered.

'Then I'm sorry I disturbed your Sunday recreation. I think, however, that after all the unfulfilled promises you made me yesterday, you owe me a little recompense, don't you, sweet Tammy?'

He took her by the shoulders before she had even guessed his intent, and stared down into her face. Fighting against the increased beating of her heart and the tremors racing through her nerves, she tried fruitlessly to escape from his powerful grasp.

'Here's something for you to compare with your upstairs visitor,' he rasped, capturing her mouth with his own. She could feel the violence in him, the taut power of his thighs pressed against hers, making her traitorous body quiver, and the bruising pressure of his hands as they left her shoulders to lace through her hair, ensuring she had no way of avoiding his brutal caress.

When it was over he left her gasping for breath, then he turned on his heel, opening the door and striding down the path without a backward glance. Fighting against the tears of rage and frustration burning her eyes, Tamar tentatively touched her throbbing lips. So Dagan Carmichael was a sore loser? But the fact was, *he* had lost their last battle. So why did she feel as if it had been she?

CHAPTER NINE

TAMAR left early for the office on Monday. On Sunday evening Pamela's mother had phoned her to say her daughter was suffering from a particularly nasty cold and wouldn't be in for a couple of days. It wasn't very nice natured of her, Tamar knew, but to be honest she welcomed Pamela's absence, feeling relieved she wouldn't have to put on an act for the younger girl. At least, now, in the privacy of the outer offices, she wouldn't have to try to assume a lightheartedness she didn't feel. Besides which, she would welcome the extra work-load. It would help to keep her mind occupied.

She had dressed carefully, wearing a dark grey tailored wool skirt suit. With its fitted waist and fashionable dropped peplum it was both smart and decorous, and the silver-grey mandarin-collared silk blouse she teamed it with helped to portray an image of cool efficiency—or so she hoped.

Early though she was, Dagan was already in his office, standing gazing down at the busy streets below with his back to her as she walked in, the white vellum envelope containing her resignation held tightly in her right hand.

For a moment she stood still, feasting her eyes on the length and strength of him, enjoying the breadth of his shoulders, the close-fitting blue shirt, sleeves rolled back to expose his tanned forearms, the closely tailored trousers with their dropped waistline and hip-hugging snugness.

He emanated a brute force, an aura of power over people's lives that terrified her as much as it attracted her. She couldn't guess his thoughts and she wouldn't want to try.

'Tammy.' He turned and smiled at her, a soft twist of his mouth that made the breath catch in her throat. She hadn't known what reception to expect after the way they had parted, and if she'd had to guess it wouldn't have been this low-key greeting.

She returned his smile automatically, guessing it didn't reach her eyes and knowing that for both their sakes it was sensible to pretend they had never been more than employer and employee, that there had never been a time when their bodies had hunted against each other for fulfilment.

'Good morning, Dagan.' She laid the envelope squarely on his blotter. 'This is the note I said I'd let you have.'

His glance touched it fleetingly before returning to her face. 'Won't you sit down for a moment, Tammy?' He nodded towards the chesterfield. 'I've made some coffee. I thought we could probably both do with some.'

'I've a lot to do today; Pam's away sick.' A swift colour advanced and faded from her pale face. 'If it's about yesterday, then I'm afraid there's nothing I can add.'

'But there's something I have to.' His voice brooked no opposition. 'I'm not going to pounce on you, Tammy, so please do me the courtesy of sitting down and listening.'

Reluctantly she obeyed him, accepting the coffee he poured for her with a murmur of thanks, grateful when he resumed his chair behind his desk.

'I owe you an apology,' he said crisply, 'for the way we parted yesterday. I'd like you to believe I'm not generally so crass in my behaviour. You have every right to run your private life as you see fit, and I was way out of line to comment on it, in word or in deed.'

'Thank you.' She couldn't meet his frank blue gaze, dropping her eyes to appraise the steaming coffee. 'I appreciate your saying so, but my resignation still stands.'

'I shall be sorry to lose you, but I think you're right.' Dagan's prompt agreement took her by surprise. There was no doubt they had worked well together. He'd delegated more responsibility to her than Hugh Drummond had ever thought of, and for a few seconds she had imagined Dagan's apology was the precursor of a plea for her to change her mind. Was it disappointment or relief she felt at his easy acceptance of her decision? A sinking feeling in the pit of her stomach suggested the former— not that she would have allowed herself to be persuaded. It was obvious he would find her continued presence as embarrassing as she did. History repeating itself, as she had always known it would.

'I've given the customary four weeks' notice,' she said with assumed equanimity. 'I can always leave earlier if you prefer it.'

His dark head shook. 'It will take longer to replace you than that, and you know it.' He paused to take a long draught of coffee, and she rose to her feet, cup in hand, supposing the interview was finished.

'No, wait, Tammy!' His cup hit the saucer with force. 'I agree it's impossible for us to work together as closely as we have been, and I take the blame for that, but I'm not going to see you throw away everything you've built up in this company. You're well-liked and respected, not only by your own colleagues but by the agencies who supply us with our life-blood. Have you thought any more about becoming an advertisement rep?'

'No—I . . .' She stared back at him with dazed eyes. His face was tautly controlled as his eyes flickered over her with calculated regard. 'You mean for INI?'

'It would be a solution, wouldn't it? For both of us. I wouldn't lose a member of my staff I value highly, and you wouldn't be throwing away your talents and experience on a matter of principle. In fact, you'd be taking steps on the road to a career which could lead to management, and if you decided you didn't like it—well, I'm prepared to get a temporary girl in here and you can always come back to secretarial work when I've left.'

Tamar stared back at him, blindingly aware that what he was saying made sense.

Dagan watched her, waiting for an answer, and when it didn't come he rose impatiently from his chair.

'Of course you'd still be working under my direction and we'd see each other regularly, but not on a day-to-day basis as before, and not in isolation. You'd report primarily to Mike Redway and be answerable first to him for results.' He paused, a slight smile touching his sensuous mouth. 'Would you give it a go, Tammy, or can't you even bear to be under the same roof as me?'

Tamar hesitated, her first instinct to turn the proposition down, logic telling her she would recover from his effect on her more easily if she never set eyes on him again. But it was a powerful lure, and the idea of hedging her bets, leaving the door open to return to her present job on Dagan's departure, was attractive.

'Any comments?' He moved across the room to take her cup and saucer from her hand. He was so close in that moment of leaning over her that she caught the scent of his skin mixed with the aura of clean linen and expensive cologne. She closed her eyes, blotting out his image as he walked away.

'It seems a reasonable compromise.' Her decision made, she spoke firmly, keeping her voice coolly emotionless.

'Then I won't need this.' With an air of triumph Dagan lifted the envelope from his desk and handed it back to her. 'Four weeks from now you start your new job. In the meantime, you'd better start searching for a temporary secretary for me—and make sure she's good. She's got a hard act to follow!' He turned from her to pick up a pile of folders on his desk, summarily dismissing her from his presence. She went with mixed feelings, still uncertain whether she had made the right decision, but determined not to let him see her doubts.

Two weeks later she was just as unsure. It had been a gruelling fortnight, with Dagan being stretched to the limit of his capabilities—first with trouble in the warehouse and, following that, non-co-operation from the circulation manager of one of the INI Sundays, which had ended with direct confrontation and Dagan firing him on the spot.

There was still no news on Creta, the agency having put off the presentation to client for non-specified reasons, and despite the gallant efforts of the advertising representatives they had failed to reach their monthly target for the first time since Dagan had taken over the helm.

Fiamma, emerging bright-eyed and flushed from a sudden summons to Dagan's office, made no bones about his aggressive reaction to events.

'Phew!' she exclaimed, raising elegant eyebrows high above her green eyes. 'He surely got out of the wrong bed this morning!'

'The wrong *side* of the bed, you mean, don't you?' giggled Pam.

'Side be hanged,' Fiamma retorted. 'That's one hell of a frustration that's being indulged in there.' She indicated his door with a nod of her bright head. 'Someone's given him a bad time, and I admit to a sneaking regard for her, whoever she is! It can't be easy to turn someone like Lover Boy down!' She gave a wicked, dimpling grin. 'Trouble is, I opened my big mouth and told him he should look elsewhere for his relaxation if she wasn't coming across.'

'Oh, Fiamma!' Pamela was horrified.

Tamar regarded the shapely redhead with undisguised admiration and not a small qualm of apprehension. 'How did that go down?'

'Not very well,' Fiamma admitted with a shrug. 'He told me I should look for a job elsewhere.'

Pamela's dark eyes grew round with horror. 'Did he mean it?'

Fiamma shrugged again. 'He's given me three months to double my conversion figures—or else.' She tossed the wealth of flame-coloured hair. 'I guess he meant it all right.'

For once Tamar was out of the firing line and grateful for it. Having told Pamela of Tamar's decision, Dagan had announced his intention of passing a lot of the work through the younger girl, so that when an eventual senior replacement was found she would be able to be of more help to her, and at the same time advance her own career prospects. It was a decision Tamar had greeted with relief. The less she was in Dagan's presence, the more able she was to cope with the situation.

If she had needed any proof that his affair with Carrie was active, it would have been provided the night a plane belonging to a major international airline crashed in Japan. It so happened the INI daily was carrying a full-page advertisement for the airline in question. As was policy in such emergencies, the advertisement was taken out on the authority of the night editor, and Dagan was phoned at one-thirty in the morning and told as a matter of courtesy. When a woman's sleepy voice answered the phone in Dagan's bedroom, the office gossips had a field day. Tamar had tried to pretend to herself that she didn't care—but not with a marked degree of success.

So it was with a feeling of apprehension that she entered his office in answer to his summons with only two more weeks to spend as his secretary.

'I'm organising a seminar in Gloucester for the end of this week,' he began without preamble as soon as she had closed the door behind her, 'on behalf of all the INI titles.' He was sitting, one lean hip perched on his desk, jacketless and with his shirt-sleeves folded high on his muscular arms. His deep-sea-coloured eyes fastened on and held her lighter gaze.

'You probably know the kind of thing I mean. It's an opportunity to get a group of representatives together working as a team, under one roof, and away from family responsibilities and any other personal activities that might distract them.'

She murmured her assent as he continued unhurriedly, 'It consists of lectures, study groups, brainstorming sessions and an introduction to elements of newspaper production and management many of them are unfamiliar with. They'll be set problems and expected to come up with the answers.' He paused momentarily. 'I want you to be there, Tammy. I think you'll find it a rewarding experience.' He waited expectantly, one long leg swinging idly.

'It sounds exciting,' she said honestly. 'When does it start, and for how long?'

'Sunday to Saturday midday.' He shifted his position slightly, reminding her of a jungle cat primed to attack if the necessity arose, forcing her unwillingly to recognise that he still possessed the power to unsettle her, even in this impersonal approach. 'I would be obliged, though, if in the circumstances you could leave the rest of the last Saturday and the whole of Sunday free,' he continued smoothly as her eyebrows rose in surprise. 'I know it's a lot to ask, but as I shall be dispensing with your secretarial services over the period, I may need your expert help over the weekend. There'll be reports to be done, assessments to be made and documented—on overtime rates, of course. The conference is being held in a converted Georgian mansion standing in several acres of grounds, and I understand the accommodation is first class. So if you feel able to spare so much of your time, I shall be grateful.'

He was bland and distanced, and the pain of his detachment was achingly difficult for her to bear.

'Of course,' she told him quietly after a moment's thought. 'I do have a date, but I can break it for business.'

'Good.' For a moment she fancied a gleam of triumph in the darkness of his deep-set eyes. 'You'd better come to the meeting in the reps' room tomorrow at three, and I'll let you have a printed prospectus with full details.' He dismissed her with a curt nod, rising from the desk to pick up his telephone.

He had no need to look so smug, she thought wearily. She had only been going to spend the weekend with her mother and sister Ruth.

The course proved hard work but extremely stimulating, giving her the opportunity she needed to immerse her mind in other things rather than allowing it to dwell on her ill-conceived love for Dagan Carmichael.

There were moments, however, when she wished he hadn't chosen to play such a large part in the proceedings himself. It wasn't as if his presence was essential, she thought irritably. Not only did INI employ full-time tutors for the course, but they invited lecturers from outside companies as well, yet Dagan constantly outshone them all, and Tamar knew she wasn't the only person present who thought so.

His lectures were consistently excellent—pithy and controversial, stirring up old ideas of selling and presenting new angles on old problems. She had to admit his success was well-deserved. He had mastered the skills of both management and actual performance, which together made him into the formidable power he was within Conte's empire. But to sit there watching him perform was a special kind of agony when every bone in her body still ached for his forbidden caress.

Still, the seminar was one of the most exciting projects in which she had ever been included, she decided, fired with enthusiasm, and the fact it was all work and no play worried her not at all.

In that, she appeared to be alone.

'Good grief!' Fiamma confided to her after the morning session on Friday. 'I can't wait for the party tonight, so I can let my hair down. I'm not used to such concentrated effort.'

Tamar grinned at her attractive companion. Despite the pressure they had all been under, Fiamma remained cheerfully incorrigible, and Tamar suspected Dagan had a personal weakness for the fiery redhead, despite her knack of needling him, using her potent sex appeal as a weapon to oppose him.

Earlier that morning had been a typical example, as Dagan had pounced on the ex-actress as she had sat running her tongue round her dewy lips, gazing out at the weak late February sunshine.

'Fiamma,' he had asked gently. 'Perhaps *you* can tell us exactly what a "Response Function" is?'

She had been miles away, not hearing a word of his explanation on how to evaluate the results of computer analyses of advertising schedules. He had stood there, very sure of himself, trying to embarrass her by drawing attention to her distraction.

'Well now, Dagan,' she had drawled, putting the end of her pen daintily in her mouth and nibbling it thoughtfully, without any sign of being discomfited, 'I could surely come up there with you now and *demonstrate* it!'

There had been laughter from the predominantly male audience, a couple of catcalls and a shout of 'Attagirl!' as Fiamma had allowed her beautiful green eyes to travel the lean length of Dagan's relaxed body, dwelling with unmitigated delight on his long, hard thighs encased in tight, smooth denim, his flat abdomen and broad shoulders beneath his casual cotton shirt, before coming to rest contemplatively on his attractive face, daring him to be angry with her.

He hadn't been.

'I may take a rain-check on that offer,' he'd murmured, his eyes darkening with amusement before moving them to rest thoughtfully on Tamar, who was seated beside her. 'In the meantime, perhaps Tammy can enlighten us on the subject.'

It had been so much like being in school, she'd had to fight the urge to stand up in her place and call him Sir. Annoyingly aware that her voice had shaken nervously as she had told him, 'It's a subjective table of values given by an advertiser to individual exposure levels of advertising,' she hadn't even dared to meet his faintly quizzical, superior smile. She'd only relaxed when he'd said pleasantly, 'Yes, admirably paraphrased, Tammy. I can see you at least have been paying attention.'

She'd been pleased with his praise, even though it had been slightly patronising, but she'd wished her temperament could have been more like Fiamma's. If only she'd had that carefree, irresponsible attitude towards life, she could have flung caution to the winds and let Dagan love her as he had wanted, as she had wanted...

'What are you going to wear tonight?' Fiamma broke into Tamar's recollections, dragging her mind back to the present.

'Why, nothing spectacular. It's not dressy, is it?' she asked anxiously, aware she had only packed a couple of day dresses, not anticipating the farewell party which had been announced.

'Well, the men are wearing lounge suits, and I don't suppose a little glamour will go amiss. Tell you what,' Fiamma linked her arm through Tamar's, 'I couldn't make up my mind, so I packed a couple of dresses. I've decided on the gold, so I'll lend you the scarlet.' Her practised eye travelled over Tamar's body. 'You're a size twelve too, I can see—and you won't have to put tissues in the bra cups as I do!'

'Oh, I don't know—' Tamar hesitated. 'Won't we be overdressed?'

'No, darling!' Fiamma said firmly. 'Whatever else, not that!'

Leaving Fiamma's room at seven that evening, Tamar knew precisely what Fiamma had meant. The scarlet dress was made of silk jersey, it's only claim to modesty being a soft built-in bra. For the rest, it was a tube of slinky stretch material, held on the shoulders by shoestring straps, defying the law of gravity by its ability to cling like a second skin to the female form.

'But I can't wear this!' gasped Tamar. 'You'll be able to see my underclothes!'

Fiamma had flicked her a disparaging look. 'You're not supposed to be wearing any, silly!' Then, as she had seen the expression on her colleague's face, 'OK, OK, so compromise. Haven't you got any thin nylon pants without lace or pattern? For heaven's sake, darling, the place is centrally heated; you won't catch pneumonia!' Her voice had suddenly gentled as she had given Tamar a slow, knowing wink, not without compassion. 'But you might just catch your heart's delight.'

Shocked, Tamar had tried to bluff. 'I don't know what you mean!'

'Of course you do,' the redhead had returned kindly. 'Don't get so upset. I've trodden the same path many times—oh, not with Dagan Carmichael, but I know the symptoms.'

It was useless to pretend with Fiamma. How right Dagan had been when he had acknowledged her perspicacity. 'He's already living with a woman,' she had said, trying to sound as if she didn't give a damn.

'So they say.' Fiamma shrugged her shoulders. 'But she's not here with him tonight, is she? And you are. Besides which, our Dagan's a bit of a dark horse. He doesn't wear his heart on his sleeve, but I've been watching him when he least suspects it, and I'd say you've got a fabulous chance of getting him between the sheets—if that's what you want.'

'It's not!' Quickly Tamar denied it, guessing she wasn't fooling the other girl and certain she wasn't fooling herself. Dear heavens, if only she could feel Dagan's lips on her own once more. If she could touch him, savour his nearness. She was starving for him, but common sense told her he couldn't be on her diet. She had made her decision. She was being absurd to question its wisdom.

Yet was she being stupid in taking such a strong stand? Was it so wrong to indulge in a few hours' casual love-making with a man one loved? Was the pain of losing him going to be that much harder if they had been lovers? Yes, she had to admit, it probably would be. Besides, there was Carrie. However long a leash the spectacular blonde kept Dagan on, she, Tamar, had too much pride to be taken just because she made herself available. Besides, who was to say that Fiamma's view of things was the correct one? It was more than probable that Dagan had lost patience with her and wouldn't accept her now even if she offered herself to him on a plate. Not when he had so many other options open to him.

Fiamma gave her a shrewd look, but with unusual tact forbore to comment further.

When the two girls entered the dining-room, it was to discover the formal meal had been abandoned in favour of a buffet, low lights and middle-of-the-road disco music, played slightly softer than usual to allow for conversation.

Although there had only been a handful of women on the course, they had been joined by several of the administrative staff attached to the centre so that the male/female ratio was better adjusted. Fortunately for Tamar's peace of mind, most of the women were wearing party dresses, although none perhaps quite so outstandingly so as herself and Fiamma, but the atmosphere was relaxed and friendly and she soon found herself enjoying the proceedings.

Standing in a group of people, ostensibly listening to Terry Lester describing an amusing incident at one of his agencies, her mind was elsewhere, as her eyes searched the room for Dagan. There would be no harm in dancing with him if he asked her, would there? In fact, it would seem strange if she refused such an invitation. The temptation to be held once more in his arms was a powerful force inside her, her imagination stimulated by Fiamma's comments.

Her ears deaf to the conversation around her, she tortured herself with the questions which still continued to plague her. Had Dagan finally accepted that she wanted nothing more to do with him, she wondered, or was the other girl right? If she did change her mind, would he still want her? Perhaps she should have let him explain about Carrie, perhaps the affair was on its way out...

Dear lord, what was she doing? Flustered by the way her thoughts were tending, Tamar helped herself to a glass of wine from a passing waiter, drinking it in two cool swallows. If national newspaper executives had groupies, *she* certainly wasn't going to be numbered among them!

At that point she saw Dagan, glimpsed his dark head above the others as he came into the room. Moving slightly, she saw he was wearing a light grey suit and felt her heart plummet alarmingly just at the very sight of him. And then she saw the woman at his side. It was so unexpected, so shattering in its implication, she felt she had been slapped in the face. So she was being illogical—but love had no logic and the truth was, the evening had just been ruined for her.

Dagan's companion was brown-haired and curvaceous, looking very small against her escort's towering six feet plus. She also had a lovely face with breathtaking dark eyes and a wide, generous mouth. Something about her reminded Tamar of Pamela. Perhaps it was just the colouring, or the look of devotion in her smile. Whatever it was, it was clear she intended to monopolise Dagan for the evening—and equally apparent that he didn't mind one bit! It wasn't the first time she'd looked forward to dancing with him, only to be rejected, but the bitterness was equally acrid.

'Dance, Tammy?' At her side Terry had stopped talking and was looking for action.

'Love to!' She pressed herself into his arms, giving herself up to the beat of the music. When that dance ended, she had another glass of wine and danced with him again. Then with someone else, then Terry once more. After that she lost count, but she was never at a loss for partners. As the champagne flowed and the party swung, Tamar swung with it.

From time to time her eyes went to the corner of the bar where Dagan sat surveying the proceedings with a benign eye. On more than one occasion she fancied he returned her gaze, expressionlessly watching her twist and cavort. On such occasions she swung her hips and slid her body sinuously to the disco beat, smiling up at her partner, whoever he was. If Dagan thought for one moment that she regretted her decision, she would make quite sure she disillusioned him. She was having a great time and she hoped he recognised it!

It was well past midnight when she subsided on a chair, her face flushed, experiencing a strange mixture of sensations. She felt fizzy and excited as well as miserable. Where was Fiamma? A steady look round the room showed no sign of the glamorous redhead—or of John Cavendish, with whom she had been dancing most of the evening. Tamar grimaced to herself. It seemed that her friend had won her heart's delight and was continuing the party privately and more intimately elsewhere.

'You all right, Tam?' It was Terry again, casting her a sympathetic look. 'You look a bit fazed.'

'It's been a long hard day.' She smiled brightly up at him. Terry would never understand how she felt. He had a lovely wife and two young children, unrequited love was well outside his experience. 'I think I'll call it a night.'

'How about a breath of fresh air first?' he asked gently. 'It's very warm in here and the wine's been flowing very freely. I could do with a breather myself. What do you say?'

Picking up her clutch-bag, Tamar rose to her feet. Bless Terry—he thought she'd had a bit too much to drink, and if the truth were told he could be right! Probably was right, if the way she stumbled slightly as she moved forward was anything to go by.

'Here, take it steady.' He placed a firm arm round her waist. 'I guess we've all been under a bit of strain these past few days, and it's beginning to tell.'

How right he was! It had been an exciting and enjoyable week in many senses. She had learned a great deal, not the least about the psychological make-up of people—what caused them to respond to advertisements, how copy was linked to their dreams, their images of themselves.

She'd been forced to take a long look at herself, what she wanted and the likelihood of achieving it. And it had all served one purpose—to confirm the fact that she loved Dagan Carmichael. Despite Carrie, despite the unknown brunette at the bar, despite his total unsuitability to her way of life or her ideals, she loved him. She couldn't explain it logically, but she knew it in every bone of her body, every heartbeat, every tear she was going to shed when she reached the seclusion of her own room.

She'd fooled herself into believing she could have the best of both worlds, circulating in the same environment without getting too close to him. It was a fallacy. The only way to get him out of her system was a good clean break. This time she wouldn't be deterred. She would give him her notice here, now, tonight. She would push it under his door, and leave the next morning, before he could speak to her. She would forfeit a month's money and make her departure instant. That way, she wouldn't have to bear the pain of having to see him again.

He didn't look up as she approached the door still with Terry's supporting arm around her, and there was something about the intimacy of his shared conversation with his girlfriend which prevailed on her not to interrupt. She moved silently past him, her heart twisting with regret that she hadn't even been able to wish him a last goodnight.

CHAPTER TEN

IT TOOK Tamar longer to compose the short note than she had expected, because tears kept blurring her vision. Dagan mustn't think she was ungrateful for the chance he had offered her, but at the same time she had to make her notice final and committing. In the end she kept it pleasant and to the point, saying she'd enjoyed working for him and appreciated his support in trying to help her change the line of her ambition, but that after the seminar she had decided she wasn't really cut out for a selling career. At the same time, she'd found the course stimulating, and now felt her future career lay in the direction of advertising agencies rather than the media.

She read it through three times, until she was finally satisfied that it gave the unemotional impression she intended. Reading between the lines, Dagan would probably think she was turning to Neil for a job. He would be wrong. Neil's position as son of the managing director of Hathaway Childs would surely grant her an entrée, but she wanted to apply and be accepted somewhere on her own merit. Where, at the present time, she hadn't decided, but her next step would be to accept her sister's long-standing invitation to spend a week with her down at Bournemouth. Nothing could be more guaranteed to act as a balm on her troubled spirit than the happy atmosphere of Ruth's home and the peaceful beauty of the surrounding countryside.

She dated her note, signed it, then before she could change her mind she walked down to the floor beneath, kneeling on the thick carpet outside Dagan's room, and

began to push the envelope through, gritting her teeth
with irritation as the equally thick carpet in the interior
of the room balked her purpose. She was so intent on
the task in hand that, when the door suddenly opened
and a strong arm lifted her round the waist and pro-
pelled her into the room, she was too surprised to
struggle.

Confused that Dagan had discovered her, she sat
shaking with reaction on the bed where he had deposited
her, while he walked back to the door, picked up the
letter and re-entered the room, kicking the door closed
behind him.

Unable to speak, she watched in silence as he opened
the envelope and absorbed the message that lay inside
it, breathing a sigh of relief as silently he refolded the
paper. Then he walked over to the bedside-table and
dropped it beside his wallet. At least he wasn't going to
challenge her decision this time.

Slightly shakily she rose, very aware of his potent,
almost hostile masculinity as he moved to stand between
herself and the door, barring her way.

'I—I didn't mean to disturb you. It's just that, having
made my decision, I thought I should get it over with
tonight,' she offered a little desperately, unnaccountably
quailing as he moved closer and placed his hands on her
bare shoulders.

'I think you should get it over with tonight, too,' he
said, a menacing harshness in his tone. 'And you do
disturb me, Tamar—you disturb me very much!'

'Yes, well...' His closeness was suffocating her, causing
the blood to pound in her ears and her senses to reel.
She twisted her head round towards the en-suite
bathroom. 'Shouldn't you—I mean won't you...?'

Irritated by his blank stare, she said impatiently, 'Oh, heavens, you know what I mean! Haven't you got a friend in there?'

'A *what*?' he bellowed, his fingers tightening threateningly on her arms. 'What the hell are you on about now, Tamar?'

He was enraged, and the fact that she no longer worked for him didn't seem to alter her reaction to the fact. She had to fight hard to keep her composure, but she was no fool. Since Dagan hadn't had time to drive his ladyfriend back whence she came, it was only reasonable to assume she was still on the premises—and where better than his executive suite?

Imitating the sophisticated smile she had seen so often on Fiamma's gamine features, she said smoothly, 'I'm afraid I assumed your companion at the bar would be sharing your bed tonight.'

'Did you, by heaven!' He was looking at her strangely, with a distinctly unfriendly gleam in his eyes. 'As you're so interested in my social life, let me tell you about Gina. About four years ago I came over here to look over a Scottish media group Conte was interested in, and stayed for about a year to do a feasibility study. At the time, Gina was my secretary. She'd recently married and was very concerned because her husband had been made redundant. It so happened I was able to get him fixed up with something.'

In a clipped lecturer's tone he continued briskly, 'They were—are—a very nice young couple. They've recently moved from Scotland and live a couple of miles away from this place. When Gina read in the local paper that INI were holding a seminar here, she phoned me. I invited both her and her husband over tonight, but she came alone because he was baby-sitting with their twins.

'She's an intelligent, lively girl and I enjoyed her company. I was pleased to hear how successful Bill is now and how well the children are thriving. About ten minutes ago, when her younger brother returned from the cinema, he took over the baby-sitting and Bill came and collected his wife and took her home to her own bed.'

The whole explanation had been delivered in a cool, matter-of-fact voice, as if she'd been entitled to hear it, but she knew him too well to be deceived by his apparent calmness. Underneath, Dagan Carmichael was simmering like an active volcano, and Tamar hoped desperately that she would be out of his path by the time the explosion took place.

'Well?' he asked with deceptive gentleness. 'Any questions?'

'No.' She shook her head miserably, angry that he had made her feel ridiculous. Some latent sense of pride forced her into contention. 'But I can't really be blamed for what I thought,' she muttered, her grey eyes flickering round the room, encompassing the couch, the armchairs and standard-lamp, the whole magnificent size of the room. 'After all, it is a double room, isn't it?'

His blue eyes darkened ominously. 'And after all, I am a bloody director!' he gritted. 'The hell—you expect me to sleep in the basement?'

'I suppose not,' she mumbled ungraciously, wanting only to escape. 'I'm sorry if my jumping to conclusions offended you. Now I've given you my letter, I'll be getting back to my own room.'

'Your room?' Now it was Dagan's turn to express polite disbelief. 'Come now, Tamar, that get-up wasn't put on tonight so you could go back alone to your own room.' His piercing gaze seemed to strip her as it lingered on every outlined curve and hollow of her body. 'Or are you expecting to find a dozen or so of my staff queuing up outside?'

'You're disgusting!' she spat back, antagonised by his contempt. The whole scene was too redolent of the aftermath of Martin Sanders' attempted seduction to be bearable. Fury giving her an added strength, she dislodged her captive arm, raising her hand. Dagan was ready for her, catching her wrist before she could land a blow on his darkly saturnine face.

'Sauce for the goose, sweetheart!' He seized the other wrist as well, holding them down at her sides and pulling her body very close to his own. 'That resignation was dated yesterday. You're no longer my employee, and I can pay you back in your own coin without the fury of the unions descending on my head.' He paused, his voice thick with temper. 'Lay a finger on me and I'll pay you back with interest—though not necessarily in the same coin. Haven't you caused me enough trouble already, throwing aside the arrangements I made for you, walking out on me after agreeing to stay on to sort out the clerical implications of what's been achieved? At the moment I would very much enjoy an excuse to teach you one more lesson to add to those you've already learned over the past week!'

Tamar stared at his angry face, mutiny on every line of her own, but she didn't dare to raise her hand to him again, although her palm itched to wipe the sardonic sneer from his lean features. Discretion told her he was making no idle threat, and her own conscience told her that from his point of view she had behaved irresponsibly—but then, he couldn't know the extent of the emotional upheaval he had caused in her ordered life.

When he realised he'd made his point, he released her wrists, pushing her gently so that she sank down again on the edge of the bed. Standing looking down at her, his eyes darkening, his mouth unsmiling, he made a forbidding picture.

'Why did you wear that dress, Tamar?'

'I don't know what you mean. It was a party, wasn't it?' Suddenly she felt very vulnerable. With Fiamma beside her she had felt no qualms. Now, with Dagan's impertinent eyes resting on the exposed curve of her pale breasts, she felt uneasy.

'Are you wearing anything at all underneath it?'

She sucked in her breath in dismay. 'How dare you ask me that?'

He shrugged careless shoulders. 'It was what every other man in the room wanted to know,' he told her casually. 'You can't be that naïve.'

'I'm adequately clothed.' Her voice shook, partly because she resented his taking her to task, and partly because he was resurrecting her initial apprehension. She had been foolish to be guided by Fiamma. They were, after all, two quite different types.

'To be seduced, perhaps,' he agreed drily. 'Have you any idea at all what it does to a man to see a woman dressed as you are, behaving as you did, when he suspects that under the visible covering she's stark naked?'

Tamar bit her lip, refusing to meet his eyes. Why should she be responsible if men had fantasies? Women were entitled to dress to please themselves.

Dagan sighed, and she couldn't be certain whether he was losing patience or humouring her. 'I'd be very surprised if it's part of your own wardrobe.'

'I chose to wear it,' she said firmly. 'And I haven't the slightest intention of apologising for my decision. Besides,' she shot him a withering look, 'if I'd thought about it at all, I would have supposed *you* would have liked it!'

'Oh, I would,' he shot back, a tremble of laughter in his voice now. 'If you were in my home and I'd come back after a bad day in the office and you greeted me at the front door dressed like that, I'd like it very much indeed!'

The atmosphere in the room was dangerously charged. Every instinct told Tamar she must get out while she still could. Oh, why hadn't she been able to slip that wretched note under the door without his seeing? Without the bond of working for him, she had no claim on his protectorship. She was on new and uncertain ground, where a false move could be disastrous.

'Well, I'm not,' she said briskly. 'And you're not either. So, since you find the sight of me so displeasing, I'll wish you goodnight.' She made a move to stand up.

'Stay where you are!' barked Dagan. Surprised, she subsided, feeling her pulse increase its rhythm as he sank down beside her on the bed, his hand resting gently on her jersey-covered knee. The long slit of the dress parted, revealing her naked thigh. She made no move to cover it, sitting rigid, staring straight ahead as he took his time studying the long, sweeping curves of her shapely legs.

'You really put yourself on show this evening, didn't you, Tammy?' His voice was conversational, but with dark, indefinable undertones colouring it. 'Who for, I wonder? Not Cavendish—his hands are full with Fiamma!'

Tamar bit her lip in chagrin. Fiamma had been discreet, but she hadn't fooled Dagan.

'You danced with Lester a lot,' he mused. 'But he's a devoted family man. You'd be wasting your time there.'

'Stop it, Dagan!' she blurted out, turning her head away so that he wouldn't see the tears forming in her eyes.

'Why did you really come to my room?' his soft voice persisted as his hand moved to encircle her waist. She could feel the heat of his body burning through the thin material of her dress. Despite her anger and the element of fear his nearness engendered, she was reacting to his magic, her body changing beneath his touch with frightening speed, adapting itself to welcome his caresses. This was a madness from which she must free herself before she lost all self-respect.

'Answer me!' he demanded. 'You didn't have to deliver your resignation personally. You could have left it at the desk if you were too scared to face me. So why did you come, Tammy?'

Wide-eyed, she stared back into his dark face so close to her own, unable to answer. He was right—it must have been the Devil who had driven her to make the stupid mistake of going to his room.

He smiled at her shocked expression with unexpected tenderness. 'Have you changed your mind? Have you decided that Neil Hathaway can't give you everything you want—that your heart is as warm as your very lovely body, and perhaps you need someone else to take care of both of them? Is that it, Tammy? Can it be that you've decided you want me, after all? Is that the real reason you've resigned—because now we no longer work for the same company you can indulge your desires and still keep your principles?'

'No! I don't want you!' she cried out in an agony of passion. 'I never really wanted you!' She was lying to salvage her pride, even while her skin burned beneath the gentle movement of his fingers. It would be an insult to what she felt for him to allow herself to become just another of his diversions.

'Didn't you?' he drawled softly. 'I seem to remember differently.' The hands round her waist moved to her shoulders, lowering the delicate straps. His dark head dipped towards her, allowing his lips to follow the slight impression they had left on her soft skin, while she sat spellbound, wanting to move, but frozen by the conflict of her own body.

'Yes,' he concurred softly, 'I think I've defined the truth, haven't I? You did come to me tonight, Tammy, with your resignation because it absolves you from breaking the rules you've set yourself. Now you no longer work for me, there's nothing to prevent us from becoming lovers, is there?'

He pulled her dress slightly so that it stretched, then rolled off her breasts, leaving them bare and beautiful before his avid gaze. Tamar's breath jerked painfully between her dry lips, but she was powerless to move. Then Dagan lowered his head and ran the soft dampness of his lips across her tumid nipples, and she stiffened, a piercing sweetness unlocking itself deep inside her, so that she moaned faintly at the sensation he was arousing.

Dagan laughed softly, his breath warm against her naked flesh, as the soft caress of his mouth dragged itself with heavy languor across her quivering skin. 'Oh, Tammy, admit it, sweetheart, you want me as badly as I want you!'

He wanted her desperately—that was alarmingly obvious. She could feel his body trembling, sense his suppressed desire, knew by his ragged breathing that he was deeply and hotly aroused as his mouth on her breast moved more urgently, causing her to moan in a terrible agony of pleasure as its soft bud swelled to fullness within the sweetness of his lips.

There was no point in lying or clinging to rules that were suddenly meaningless, because her body had already betrayed her. Tamar felt only relief as she let the remainder of her crumbling resolutions dissolve, lifting her arms to hold him against her, cradling his head in the haven it had found, lacing her fingers through his hair, burying her face in its luxuriant darkness, inhaling the intoxicating scent of his skin.

'Yes, oh, yes, Dagan,' she confessed in a whisper. 'I want you so much!'

Gently he pushed her back on the bed, lunging for the bedside-lamp and turning it off, plunging the room into darkness. She heard rather than saw his clothes being discarded, lying where she was, breathing quickly, every nerve on edge, waiting for him to rejoin her. It was only seconds before she felt him stroking her flushed cheek with the back of his hand before he bent towards her, kissing her face tenderly, sharpening her desire, as he avoided her mouth.

'You are sure this is what you want?' It was a soft whisper as she felt the heated silk of his body touch her own.

'It's what I want...'

He kissed her deeply, satisfyingly—his mouth capturing hers as her breasts rose to greet his satiny, muscled chest. When at last he released her lips, his hands dropped to her dress. Breathing heavily and fast, he smoothed it down her body, letting out a sharp exclamation of satisfaction when his sensitive fingers touched the delicate undergarment, then he hesitated.

With an inspired certainty, Tamar knew that if at that moment she'd changed her mind, begged him to stop at that point, he would have done so. Turning her face into the softness of the pillow, she remained silent, feeling her body melting with a quivering eagerness, knowing its message would be clear and uncomplicated to a man as experienced as Dagan.

She heard him catch his breath, accepting her tacit consent as he eased the dress and the simple briefs down her body, slipping each sandal from her foot as the fabric touched them, allowing everything to fall together at the foot of the bed.

'Let me look at you.' His voice was cloaked in reverence. Now her eyes had grown accustomed to the dimness, Tamar could see the naked desire in his eyes, as potent an aphrodisiac as his touch to her inflamed flesh. When he lowered his head to blaze a trail of pulse-quickening caresses with his open mouth down the length of her uncovered body, she moved beneath him, languid with delight.

'Oh, my darling.' His deep voice, vibrant with desire, caressed her and she felt the pitch of his excitement increase at her response. She smiled in the darkness as he drew seductive hands over her smooth skin, exploring with a tender sensitivity the secrets of her warm, damp body, way past the point where taking her first lover worried her.

What she didn't know, Dagan would teach her; but she was so physically and mentally ripe for fulfilment that he might not even realise she was a virgin, particularly since she had let him believe she'd spent the night with Neil.

A woman's inexperience wasn't always obvious to a man, especially in a joint moment of soaring passion...and that was what it would be, she thought exultantly, nuzzling Dagan's beautiful firm mouth, teasing his lips with gentle kisses, before trailing her fingers with a deadly purpose across his smooth chest, locating the hard nub of his male nipples and bestowing on them the pleasure of her tongue.

With a dreadful joy she touched his body, sweeping her fingers with trembling excitement over his lean ribs, sliding downwards, rejoicing in the half-smothered moans of pleasure and anguish she was evoking, fondling his fine male body for his pleasure and her own joy, guided by the rapture of his positive response.

His eyes were shuttered, his mind awash in sensual pleasure, yet a spark of awareness had fastened his gaze on her face, seeing and desperately excited by her physical pleasure in him. Head thrown back, lips parted, her breath coming hard and fast, Tamar slid her hands across his trembling flesh until she held him balanced on a pinnacle of craving.

She hadn't expected him to react to her touch like this. She had anticipated some kind of master performance, polished and controlled. Now she realised with pride and awe the power she could command as a woman, and was both humbled and delighted by it.

Sensing Dagan's control was on a knife-edge, she drew his dark head towards her breast, guiding its fullness to his mouth once more, wanting to feel a part of her body inside him, before she took him to herself, absorbing his sweetness and strength.

With eyes dreamy and dazed, he moved to cover her body, hands on the pale sheets beside her shoulders. When he spoke, it was with a voice husky with emotion, heavy with a plea for clemency.

'Carrie,' he gasped. 'Oh, Carrie! Don't make me wait for you any longer. Carrie, I have to take you now...'

Ice being thrown over her couldn't have shocked or distressed her more. Tamar moaned in protest as shock, frigidity and pain froze her body. She had managed to put Carrie out of her mind, deliberately fooled herself into believing that the glamorous blonde had magically disappeared from his life. Now she had been disillusioned in the cruellest way possible.

To be a warm body in a bed and to be called by another woman's name was unbearable! Dagan and she had worked together for months. She was no stranger picked up in a bar or off the street. Damn him! The least he could have done at the sweet moment of culmination was to remember her name!

Outrage lent her a formidable strength as she escaped from his weight, using her fists and her nails, her elbows and knees, rolling out of the bed on to the floor. Shaking uncontrollably, she felt feverishly for her discarded dress, locating it quickly and pulling it over her trembling body as harsh sobs strangled in her throat.

To Dagan, her seduction would have been one of many similar experiences. To her, it would have been the first, and she was not going to allow another woman's name to be on his lips at the moment of her surrender!

'What's wrong?' Dazed and shaken, Dagan was regarding her like a man suddenly awakened from the dead. Tamar hoped he felt as dreadful as she did. No—worse! In the semi-darkness, he couldn't catch the venom in the look she flashed him, but he knew the spell was broken.

'What's wrong?' he asked again, sounding perplexed and confused. 'I wouldn't have hurt you, Tammy. I swear I'd never do anything to hurt you.'

Now it was too late, he remembered who she was! Tamar's body felt weak and unfulfilled, her legs rubbery, her movements uncoordinated.

Not trusting herself to speak, she settled the straps of her dress, found the flimsy briefs and screwed them up into a ball in her hand. What would it matter if anyone did see her coming out of Dagan's room in this dreadful state? She was no longer a part of the zany, amoral crowd who had been her friends and colleagues. She had never judged them, only known that their way could never be hers. Tonight had proved that belief beyond any possible doubt.

'Tammy!' Dagan had risen from the bed and thrust his powerful legs into trousers. Unclasped and unzipped, they clung to his lean hips, giving him a misleading aura of respectability. 'For pity's sake, talk to me! What went wrong?' He sounded hurt and bewildered rather than furious, as she would have expected.

Turning at the door, Tamar drew in her breath, choosing only to comment on his earlier plea.

'Hurt?' she contested bitterly, staring him full in the face, imprinting his imperious features on her memory in one last agonising act of betrayed love. 'You've hurt me more than anyone else in my life!'

The following moments remained a blur. Somehow she regained her room and went through the motions of washing her face, brushing her teeth and peeling off Fiamma's infamous dress, before crawling naked between the sheets, surviving the remainder of the night between periods of uneasy sleep and stretches of miserable wakefulness, her only wish to get away from the seminar centre as far and as soon as possible.

Fortunately she wasn't hungry, because nothing would have persuaded her to go down to breakfast. The thought of seeing her colleagues was bad enough, the thought of seeing Dagan was intolerable.

As soon as was reasonable she phoned the reception desk and found the time of the first train back to London from the local station, ordering a cab to come for her at ten o'clock—half an hour before its departure.

She waited until the morning session was well under way before carrying her case downstairs, praying she wouldn't encounter Dagan along the way. She didn't. But she did see him a few minutes later.

She was sitting in a large armchair in the main lounge when he walked past the open door on his way to reception. She cowered back in her chair, afraid he might glance in her direction, but he passed by whistling softly between his teeth, apparently at peace with the world.

It was purgatory to look at him, but she couldn't take her eyes away, watching while he spoke to the receptionist. He was wearing light blue jean-cut trousers styled with a close tailoring that enhanced his lithe body, emphasising its animal grace and agility, and a chunky knitted navy sweater stretched smoothly over his hard-muscled chest, causing Tamar's heart to ache with a fierce sense of loss.

He had his back to her now, leaning forward, talking earnestly, and Tamar saw the girl nod and stroke her own hair in a preening gesture. Then he turned, folder in hand, and took the stairs that led to the conference room two at a time without a glance in her direction.

Heaving a sigh of mingled relief and despair, Tamar looked away. That was the very last time she would ever set eyes on Dagan Carmichael, for by the time she left he would be well and truly launched into the final lecture of the seminar.

She helped herself to a handful of magazines from a nearby table, leafing through them, staring sightlessly at *Punch*, finding herself unable to fit one clue into the *Telegraph* crossword and wondering why it was that time took so long to pass when one was miserable. It was with the utmost relief she sprang to her feet when the receptionist arrived to tell her the car she had ordered had arrived.

She was so deep in thought as she carried her weekend case out on to the forecourt, that she didn't even look at the vehicle parked outside. It was only as she bent to open the door that she realised Dagan was in the driving seat and recoiled in horror.

'You're giving a lecture!' she accused him nonsensically, flushing scarlet with rage and mortification that he had forced her to face him again.

'My ubiquity is part of my charm,' he said, obviously amused by her absurd remark. 'The secret of success is getting one's priorities right—and knowing when to delegate. I decided to let Terry Lester wind up the proceedings for me.' He reached out an imperative hand. 'Give me your case, Tammy. I'll put it on the back seat.'

Heart thumping nineteen to the dozen, a desperate weakness invading her limbs, Tamar stared back at him, trying to read the bland expression on his face, her eyes widening in an unspoken appeal to leave her alone, to allow her the opportunity of disappearing from his life with some dignity.

'No, no, I can't,' she refused curtly. 'I'm expecting a car to take me to the station.'

'Give me your case and get in, Tammy!' Dagan repeated firmly. 'Haven't you realised yet that *I* am the car you're expecting? It was easy to anticipate your actions, so I waited until you ordered the car and told the receptionist I'd handle it.'

'How dare you interfere?' Fury brought a flush to her pale face as the fresh breeze whipped her blonde hair against her cheeks.

'There isn't going to be another car coming for you today, so if you want to go anywhere, you'd better get in!' There was a tinge of impatience about him now as he drummed his fingers along the back of the front passenger seat.

Tamar couldn't imagine why he was doing this. It was a twenty-minute drive to the station, and what he hoped to achieve in that time was hard to imagine. She would have liked to storm away and leave him sitting there alone with the irritable frown which creased his broad forehead, but if she didn't accept his offer she was going to miss her train.

It was with a great show of reluctance that she finally handed her case over and slid into the seat beside him. This time as he leant across her he made no attempt to prevent his fingers touching her breast. Gritting her teeth, Tamar sat in silent protest as he arranged the seat-belt with meticulous care across her, before clipping it into its housing.

For the first few moments of the ride silence enveloped them, as Tamar stared resolutely out of the side window, determined not to be the first one to speak. After ten minutes, when nothing had been said, she dared to steal a sidelong glance at Dagan's profile. What she saw there made her pulse gather an erratic rhythm of its own, as messages of impending danger flashed from her bemused mind to her senses. It wasn't the first time she'd seen a similar self-satisfied expression on his face when he had been scheming some devious plan.

'You're not taking me to the station!' she accused him angrily, alerted to his intended villainy and aware for the first time that the road was unfamiliar.

'No,' he agreed calmly. 'I'm taking you home.'

'All the way to London?' Displeasure strained her voice.

'Not London. My home—Wales.'

CHAPTER ELEVEN

'WHAT?' Tamar couldn't believe her ears. 'Dagan, stop this car immediately! I've no intention of going to Wales with you!'

How dared he kidnap her in this way? She wasn't even working for him now! Her eye passed from the speedometer to the steering-wheel, realising instantly that it would be madness for her to interfere with his driving.

'Calm down, Tammy.' Dagan's slick air of natural authority did little to placate her. 'I always intended to have a long talk with you, which is why I asked you to keep today and tomorrow free. What happened last night has just precipitated matters.'

'You seem to forget that my association with INI is over.'

'I haven't forgotten,' he responded, his voice still unflurried. 'What I have to say to you is personal.'

Not deigning to reply, Tamar turned her head away from him. She couldn't stop him from speaking, but she didn't have to look at him or listen to his words.

'What you did to me last night wasn't exactly conducive to a good night's sleep,' he told her drily, pausing as if expecting some retort.

She could think of plenty. What she had done to him, indeed! What about what he had done to her? It took iron will-power to remain obdurately silent, but she had no stomach for recrimination.

'I realised it was something I'd done or said,' Dagan continued, narrowed eyes carefully fixed on the road ahead, 'but for the life of me I couldn't guess what it was. You'd been so loving in my arms, so tender to my touch. I thought, hoped I was being gentle with you—and yet you said I'd hurt you.'

Tamar let the words wash over her, refusing to turn her head or comment, angry that he was dissecting what had happened between them so cold-bloodedly.

Dagan heaved an exasperated sigh. 'Hour after hour I analysed what had happened, and it always came back to the same thing. You'd frozen me out the moment I spoke to you in Welsh.'

'You spoke to me in Welsh!' Shocked now at what seemed an outrageous, bizarre excuse, she did turn her head proudly to gaze at his stern profile, and the anger tamped away deep inside her gushed to the surface. Confident he knew exactly what he had done, what a simple but devastating error he had really made, she retorted violently, 'Your tongue certainly betrayed you! You called me...'

'*Cariad,*' he interrupted firmly. 'I called you *cariad*, Tammy—the Welsh word for beloved. Something I'd never called another woman in my life. A very special word, steeped in memories of my early childhood before that happiness was shattered. A special word,' he repeated softly. 'Just for you, Tammy—*cariad.*'

She couldn't speak, dared not believe him. Yet it could have been true. The way he said the word, putting the stress on the first syllable—*car*iad... His voice had been slurred with passion at the time, and she could so easily have misunderstood him... But did it really alter anything, anyway?

In an agony of indecision, bewildered, uncertain what to believe, her eyes stayed fastened to his face as he slowed the car down, bringing it to a halt in a clearing at the side of the winding country road on which they had been travelling.

'I wasn't sure you'd believe me,' he said cheerfully, unclipping his seat-belt and reaching to the back to lift out a plastic carrier bag from the seat. 'So I decided the best thing was to bring you to Wales and let you hear the language for yourself.'

'You're mad!' There was a tinge of hysteria in Tamar's laughter. For him to have gone to all this trouble to put the record straight... 'Quite mad!'

'So it's said of the lover, the lunatic and the poet,' Dagan agreed with good humour. 'Come along, we're going for a walk.'

Tamar followed him from the car because she had very little option and she had to admit to being intrigued by what he had just told her, not that she would allow it to influence her decision.

'It's some sort of country park,' he explained as he marched her through an avenue of leafless trees. 'It was marked on the map and I thought it would be an ideal quiet place to get things finally sorted out between us. We can sit on one of the benches and you can have breakfast and listen to what I have to say at the same time.'

Fortunately the weather was still comparatively mild for so early in the year, and despite the breeze the morning sunshine was warm on her face. It was lucky, though, that she had dressed warmly for the journey home, wearing trousers, low heels and a padded jacket, she thought wryly. She had hardly expected a country hike when she'd left the centre.

'This will do.' Dagan spread his long body comfortably on a rustic seat, guiding her down beside him. 'Really it should be a hamper with chicken in aspic and champagne,' he said, opening the plastic bag, 'but I didn't have much choice, so it's coffee and a doughnut.' Before her amazed gaze he reached into the bag and brought forth a Thermos flask and a bag containing an enormous doughnut. 'I noticed you missed breakfast.'

Torn between maintaining her dignity and refusing his offer, and a feeling of very real hunger stimulated by the delicious smell of the doughnut, Tamar wavered.

Dagan, appearing not to notice her indecision, flung his arms out across the back of the seat, splaying his long legs before him and gazing thoughtfully at the sky.

'I suppose it really started when you came to the office in your bikini,' he mused, 'and then insisted on taking a shower before starting work. Not usual behaviour for a secretary, and guaranteed to get attention.'

Having given in to the temptation of the doughnut, Tamar hesitated with it raised to her mouth. Dagan wasn't looking at her, and his comments didn't merit a reply. She decided to ignore him, letting her teeth bite with satisfaction into the sugary dough.

'But it wasn't until the Christmas dance that I actually realised it was more than a passing physical attraction I had for you,' he continued in the same conversational tone. 'Oh, Tammy, I'd never been jealous before and I didn't like the sensation one bit, I can tell you! Getting rid of young Hathaway proved no problem, and I guess I was arrogant enough to think you liked me enough for me to be able to work on it—to make you like me more.' He paused, as if expecting her to comment, but Tamar was experiencing an odd mixture of emotions that she couldn't quantify—besides which, the doughnut was not conducive to clear speech.

When Dagan spoke again his voice was softer, more directed. 'The thing is, I expected you to be experienced—and you weren't. You soon made it clear you weren't in the social swim, that casual and passing affairs weren't part of your normal life-style, and that frightened me a little, Tammy, because I wasn't prepared to offer commitment at that stage.'

'Is there a point to any of this?' Tamar found her voice, spurred to speak by the embarrassment she felt at his daring to judge and comment on her sexual experience—or rather lack of it—and her resentment at his allusion to commitment. Who had asked him for that, anyway? Not she.

'Naturally.' Dagan cast her an offended glance, dark brows furrowed above the startling clarity of his eyes. 'I rarely talk just for the sake of it!'

He smiled suddenly, leaning forward towards her, breaking the tension between them by unexpectedly touching the corner of her mouth gently with his tongue in a heart-flipping intimacy. Tamar's eyes widened at the caress, acknowledging silently the latent danger he still posed her.

'Sugar,' he murmured laconically, licking his lips as if it had been the most natural action in the world.

There followed a poignant silence in which Tamar, bereft of speech, watched him untypically struggle to find words. When he finally spoke, his voice was sheathed in pain.

'But things changed, Tammy, and very quickly. I soon discovered just how much I wanted you, and that night at the bungalow when I started making love to you, it *was* with the intention of making some commitment to you. I wanted a recognised relationship with you that would give me the right to warn other men away. I wanted to show you that you'd become a very important part of my life. Oh, yes—I wanted to make love to you, but I wanted much, much more. I wanted your laughter, your compassion, your generous nature, your gentleness, your loyalty—everything you'd already given me so freely in my role as employer. But this time I wanted it for myself: just me alone.'

Tamar flinched. How could she survive more of this torture? Couldn't he see that the last person she wanted to talk about was Carrie, and this was precisely where the conversation was leading? Dagan had called her compassionate, but her pity was limited. He couldn't expect to confess his tangled love-life to her and expect absolution!

'No,' she said desperately. 'I've heard enough...'

'I have to explain about Carrie!' Dagan gripped her arms as she would have risen to her feet.

'No!' It was almost a shout. 'I don't want to know about any of your women. I want to get back to London and find myself another job and never set eyes on you again!' She was shaking in his grasp.

He held her forcibly, thumbs pressing into her flesh. 'You have to know about Carrie,' he gritted, his face etched with anger. 'Because Carrie Denvers is nothing to me, has never been anything to me, will never be anything to me. Carrie Denvers is Adrian Conte's loving and devoted wife!'

Tamar stopped struggling and stared at him in open disbelief, trying to recall anything she had ever read about the tycoon's family. A beautiful blonde wife and two children, never photographed, hardly ever written about, but said to be a close, affectionate family. 'No,' she said, shaking her head. 'It's not true.' But a wild, tumultuous joy was beginning to spread through every cell of her body, warming it with the flames of hope.

Dagan smiled wryly. 'It's true, Tammy. Conte is a very powerful, very rich and influential man. That makes his family extremely vulnerable to kidnapping and physical threats. In Canada, Caroline and the children have twenty-four-hour-a-day protection. Adrian keeps them out of the public eye for their own safety. Against all odds, theirs is one of the happiest marriages around.' His smile deepened. 'Adrian trusts Caroline absolutely, and with justifiable faith. I've been close to the whole family for years, so it was natural that when Caroline wanted to come to England and savour the freedom she finds here, do some shopping, see some shows, Adrian should entrust her safety to me, particularly as I was living in their bungalow at the time.

'Carrie travelled incognito, as she always does, using a diminutive of her own name and her mother's family name.' He shook his head ruefully. 'I hadn't expected her until the following week.'

Totally astounded, Tamar grappled to come to terms with what she had just heard. It was unbelievable—yet surely it was too far-fetched to be a lie. But why couldn't Dagan have trusted her with the truth? Secret or not, surely he could have relied on her silence?

'At the time,' he admitted as if guessing her ambivalent thoughts, 'I was too utterly devastated by the swift change in events to explain the situation, added to which, Carrie's effusive greeting didn't help matters at all. She's just naturally theatrical, and of course she had no way of knowing what she'd interrupted. Afterwards she simply acted as hostess in her own home. It was a natural role to play.'

'Then that time when the plane crashed . . . ?' Tammy asked slowly.

Dagan shrugged, catching her drift immediately. 'The extension phone's in the main bedroom. Naturally, I moved out when she arrived. She answered it straight away without considering the implications, thinking it might be Adrian calling from Canada.'

'Why didn't you tell me, Dagan?' She shivered, as much from remembering the misery she had felt as from a sudden gust of cool wind which swept against her. 'You must have known what I imagined. If you cared as much as you say you did, couldn't you have trusted me?'

'I cared, Tammy.' His voice was harsh. 'And I did try—remember? But you didn't want to know. I came round to your place the following morning, but you'd already made your mind up and found your consolation elsewhere.' His blue eyes bore down into her. 'Can you imagine how that made me feel? I was furious that you hadn't waited for an explanation, hurt that you cared so little for me that you'd turned to Hathaway without giving me one chance to exonerate myself. I'd begun to believe that you felt something special for me because you were prepared to break all your own rules when I held you in my arms.'

'I did, I was...' Tamar placed a placatory hand on his thigh as his grip on her arms was released. 'Oh, Dagan, nothing mattered that evening except loving you—then when Carrie arrived I felt so sick, so humiliated...'

He bent his head and kissed her as she clung to him. 'I realised that afterwards when I got back to the bunga-low and simmered down a little. I told myself it was all my fault you didn't trust me, because what we needed was time to be alone together away from INI, away from Pamela and phone calls and meetings, and I hadn't been able to devote enough time to you outside office hours. That's when I decided to offer you the job as a represen-tative. I wasn't arrogant enough to think I had the power to keep you, but I knew I couldn't let you go completely from my life without a fight.

'If you accepted my suggestion, it meant we'd still be in close touch, without the day-to-day frustration of being continually in each other's company, forced to behave like friends instead of the lovers I wanted us to become. It would give me the opportunity of starting our relationship off again on a different footing—at a slower pace, so as not to scare you away.'

'I told myself I should make a clean break with you,' Tamar confessed, shaking her shining fair head, 'but I couldn't find the moral courage to turn my back on you completely.'

Dagan smiled down into her eyes. 'I'd intended to court you properly, Tammy. I was going to give you breathing-space, and then I was going to invite you out to dinner, explain about Carrie, take things easily…make time for theatres and concerts and nightclubs: give you a chance to relax instead of doing what I really wanted to, make endless passionate love to you!'

He sighed philosophically, a rueful grin jerking the corners of his sensuous mouth. 'I hoped I might be able to persuade you in time that I'm not the heartless phil-anderer I'm so often painted. And I was going to start my campaign this afternoon—which is why I asked you to stay on after the conference.' He raised his finger to trace the outline of her mouth as she gazed up at him. 'I promise you I don't make a habit of making love to my secretaries. In fact, although it will ruin my repu-tation, I confess you're the very first secretary I've ever fallen in love with!'

'Fallen in love?' Her heart in her mouth, Tamar queried the phrase, unable to believe her ears. Dagan Carmichael was telling her he *loved* her—or was it just a figure of speech?

'Love,' Dagan repeated firmly, fixing her with his bright stare, daring her to contradict him. 'Don't you know yet that you've carved out a place in my heart that no one else will ever be able to fill? I'd suspected it for a long time, but last night I was absolutely certain. When I saw you surrounded by men, dressed like a houri, displaying your enticing body, I was so livid with rage and frustration that if it hadn't been for Gina I think I would have marched you out of the room in double quick time and slapped some sense into you or ravished you!' For a moment the blue eyes glinted dangerously as he admitted, 'Probably both.'

'You had no right to interfere,' she protested quietly, an odd sensation drying her throat and causing her pulses to hammer wildly at his confession of unadulterated jealousy.

'That was my problem,' he agreed gravely. 'I wanted to have that right. If you hadn't come to my room last night, I was going to come to yours with every intention of winning it!' He drew her closer into his arms, holding her blonde head against his shoulder as his hand traversed her back. 'Give me the chance to make you forget Hathaway.' His voice was husky, his eyes hard-pupilled as he commanded her attention with a vital magnetism. 'Let me prove how much I love and need you, Tammy.'

Love, she thought, still bewildered by his intensity. He had said it again.

Pulling herself away, she stared up at his face, unashamedly caressing each strongly accented feature with the sweep of her appraisal, feeling her body soften, guessing he would perceive the effect his words had on her and not caring any more.

She wanted to let him know how much she loved him too, how, over the months of working with him, her feelings had matured far beyond that first buzz of sexual attraction, but before she could put her feelings into words he spoke again.

'Don't leave me, Tammy,' he whispered hoarsely. 'Never leave me again. I'll look after you, my darling, I promise you. But before you say anything, there's something you have to know. Just before I left the conference I learned from Adrian Conte that he wants me back in Canada in three months' time.'

'Oh, Dagan, no!' A cold horror clutched at her at the thought of losing him, making her shudder in dismay. Just when she had caught a glimpse of heaven...

'Come back to Canada with me!' He enfolded her in his arms, his open mouth plundered her senses, touching and tasting her, transmitting the growing tension that was building in his virile masculine body. 'I need you, Tammy.'

Her pleasure rose to meet his own as she returned his embrace, straining against him, slipping her hands inside his jacket. Every nerve-end prickling with desire for him, her breasts hard and aching against the warm pressure of his chest, she wanted him so much that she was close to tears. Ashamed at her weakness, she tried to laugh, but the sound she made was nearer a moan trembling in her throat as she dwelt on his imminent departure.

'Well, *cariad*?' Dagan asked raggedly, his cheek against her own. 'Am I asking too much?'

How could he ask her that with such quiet humility? Didn't he realise that she would follow him to the ends of the earth if he demanded it? Work wherever Conte sent him, as long as he wanted her with him? And afterwards? She shivered. She would find the strength to cope with afterwards when it happened.

'Won't Conte be surprised if you take your own secretary back with you?' she asked, forcing herself to speak lightly, still hardly daring to believe what she had heard.

'Secretary?' His head jerked back sharply. 'Are you joking, Tammy? I'm asking you to marry me!'

Shock stunned her. She couldn't speak, couldn't formulate a word. The relationship *she* had been thinking of didn't come with a gold wedding band and a certificate. If Dagan was teasing her, it was the most cruel thing he had ever done. Her stricken face accused him.

'For heaven's sake, don't look at me like that!' he said harshly. 'I know I'm not the kind of husband you wanted. I can't offer you the stability of living in any one place for a length of time, of being home each evening at six. I move about the world, Tammy, but unlike your father, I can take my family with me. I promise you I won't miss out on our child's birthdays because you and he will be with me wherever I am! And I shan't be a wanderer forever, either. With you at my side, I shall want to put down roots, I swear it!'

'Child?' she asked weakly.

'Why not?' he asked a shade defensively. 'Not immediately, of course, but in time. It's usual, isn't it? Don't you think I want a family of my own? A child to share the advantages I've worked for and won—a son or daughter to widen our circle of love?'

'Of course I'd like a child—children...' she began, still dazed by the power of the way he was pleading his cause when he'd already won it.

'But you don't think I'd be a suitable father?' Dagan didn't wait for her reply. 'Oh, Tammy, I'm not nearly as black as I'm painted. My amorous exploits have always been exaggerated. The truth is, success was my mistress and work my aphrodisiac. I always had my baser nature well under control until you came into my life like a breath of fresh air and reminded me of what I was missing!'

He gave an odd, disjointed laugh. 'I'm not asking you to say you love me, Tammy, but I know you want me. You told me so last night. I haven't the time left to woo you and court you as you deserve, wine and dine you and buy you roses, but I've got enough love to sustain both of us, *cariad*. All I'm asking is that you give me the chance to prove it. Marry me and I'll spend the rest of our lives courting you.'

'Dagan...' Tamar murmured his name, caressing its syllables with her tongue, slowly, as lovingly as her fingers itched to embrace the man himself. 'But of course I love you,' she told him softly, her eyes shining with the proof of it. 'I love you so much, I'll come to Canada with you on any terms you want. You don't have to marry me.'

'Oh, Tammy, *cariad*,' he whispered joyfully, the sweetest possible smile illuminating his personable face, 'but I do. Very much, I do!'

It was like being drunk, a strange half-world of fantasy where nothing could go wrong. Dagan led her back to the car and drove on, crossing the border into Wales. They stopped off at a pub for lunch, eating fresh bread spread with Welsh butter and chunks of Caerphilly cheese, which tasted like ambrosia.

Afterwards they drove in utter contentment through the beautiful scenery, talking of everything and nothing, coming by early evening to an old inn.

The room they took was flooded by the golden rays of the setting sun as they entered.

As soon as the door had closed behind the porter bringing their cases, Dagan held out his arms to her and Tamar went to him, throwing her arms round his neck, pressing herself against him, rejoicing in his nearness and his strength. Dagan might not be the nine-to-five, golf-playing-every-Saturday husband that she'd thought she'd wanted, but he was the only man in the world for her—just like her father had been the only man in the world for her mother. And she was glad, oh, so glad she had waited for a man who had possessed her heart before claiming her body. Which reminded her, there was something she had to clear up.

'Neil Hathaway...' she started, and felt Dagan tense against her.

'Doesn't matter,' he told her firmly, closing her mouth with a searching kiss.

'But,' she protested breathlessly when she could speak again, 'I want to tell you...'

'And I don't want to hear. The past is past, Tammy. No regrets, no recriminations!' He pushed her jacket from her unresisting shoulders, his hands sliding up beneath her soft wool sweater, a blissful expression smoothing out the lines of strain on his face. 'We're here together, *cariad*, the door is locked, no one knows where we are and the night has only just begun.'

Tamar sighed blissfully, spending her energy in helping Dagan to disrobe her instead of pursuing her argument. Her body ached so much for his possession, why waste time in talking? He would probably discover for himself very shortly what she had been about to tell him. And if he didn't there would be the sweet, lingering aftermath of fulfilment when she could tell him he had, like all the best dragons in legend, claimed a virgin as his prize.

'Let me.' Her eager fingers returned his compliment, her flushed face intent as the removal of his sweater revealed his beautifully muscled chest, causing a shudder of longing to ripple through her.

'Oh, Dagan,' she murmured, her insides melting deliciously as she reached for the clasp at his waist.

'Tammy.' He stilled her hands, his voice husky.

Surprised, she hesitated. He wasn't shy? He couldn't be!

'I'll do it.' Brushing her hands aside, he unclasped the catch, pulled the zip down and stepped out of his elegantly cut trousers. Laughter stirred deep down inside her as Tamar gazed on the black nylon briefs his action revealed. Emphasising every part of his very male anatomy, they bore the legend 'Get Lost'.

Desperately she choked her laughter back, going pink in the face with effort.

Dagan stood there watching her thoughtfully as she gasped in an agony of hilarity. Terrified of offending him, she begged forgiveness and understanding with her wide eyes, while her lips curled in near-hysteria.

Dagan tried to look stern, then to her relief she saw his face soften and laughter-lines crinkle at the side of his eyes.

'You're the only woman I'd let laugh at me at such a delicate moment,' he told her, trying to keep a straight face. 'You certainly knew what you were doing when you bought these, my love. I swear they've kept me celibate since the day I first wore them.'

'You mean Geraldine and Sara and Pauline never had the pleasure...' She hesitated delicately.

'I mean precisely that,' he growled. 'They were only ever friends or acquaintances from the last time I was here. I was quite fancy free—until you, with your blonde hair and grey eyes and unimpeachable virtue, began digging yourself into my heart.' He kissed her hungrily, almost punitively.'

'You could always have bought some new ones,' she suggested, teasing him. 'You didn't have to wear those!'

'Ah, but I thought you liked them,' he murmured against her mouth. 'And you were the only woman I wanted to please.'

'Then please me, Dagan,' she invited. 'Oh, please—please me!'

Their laughter mingled as Dagan lifted her and took her to the bed, rolling over with her in an ecstasy of movement and exuberance until her body felt light and wonderful, soft and empty—oh, so achingly empty!

Then Dagan touched her again, gently and purposefully and insistently, and the laughter stopped. He took her hands and taught her what he wanted, and she gave it to him because his pleasure was hers, until in mutual joy they discovered what they both wanted and shared it together.

Afterwards they lay damp flesh against damp flesh, hearts drumming, blood singing in unison. Tammy's hair was spread on Dagan's naked chest, her leg lying across his flat abdomen in an unconscious attitude of possession, when he asked softly, 'Did I hurt you?'

She shook her head.

'You should have told me.'

'I tried—remember?' She stretched voluptuously. 'I lied to you that morning when you came round to the apartment and I told you I wasn't alone.'

'Minx!' He laced his fingers through her hair. 'We shall have to do something about this problem of communication we have—which reminds me . . .'

'Yes?' Alerted by the change in his tone, Tamar raised herself on one elbow to gaze down on his mischievous face.

'Mike Redway phoned me first thing this morning. Not only have we got fifty per cent of the Creta budget, but Les Frinton has demanded that INI be used exclusively for the mini-launch of a new unisex cologne.'

'But that's marvellous!' Tamar's eyes sparkled with delight. 'Even though I no longer work for the company, I couldn't be more thrilled.'

'As to that, I've decided not to accept your notice after all,' Dagan retorted smoothly, 'since it was handed in as a result of a misunderstanding. You're going to need every penny you can earn now you're about to become a bride, and I'm not having you robbed of the biggest farewell party the company's ever funded for a trusted and popular employee. Besides, I want to keep you where I can see you for the next few weeks. So on Monday it's back to the grindstone for both of us!'

'But, Dagan——' she protested half-heartedly.

'But Dagan, nothing,' he told her firmly. 'It'll be fine, you'll see. It's only for a few weeks, Tammy, and I've grown to need you in more ways than one. And as that one will be adequately attended to after office hours, there won't be any problems, I promise.'

'Whatever do you mean?' She pretended confusion.

'Let me show you.'

Tamar made no objection. He was the boss, after all, and she was an only too willing pupil of his expertise. Imagine her ever regarding him as a rash intruder, she thought fleetingly, as he took her with him to another plane with a tender consideration that left her gasping with delight.

OCTOBER 1989 HARDBACK TITLES

——— ROMANCE ———

Bluebirds in the Spring *Jeanne Allan*	3188	0 263 12195 X
Intense Involvement *Jenny Arden*	3189	0 263 12196 8
Love Spin *Ann Charlton*	3190	0 263 12197 6
Storm Force *Sara Craven*	3191	0 263 12198 4
Taking Chances *Vanessa Grant*	3192	0 263 12199 2
Tender Betrayal *Grace Green*	3193	0 263 12200 X
Bitter Betrayal *Penny Jordan*	3194	0 263 12201 8
Passion's Far Shore *Madeleine Ker*	3195	0 263 12202 6
Man of the House *Miriam Macgregor*	3196	0 263 12203 4
Fly Like an Eagle *Sandra Marton*	3197	0 263 12204 2
Let Fate Decide *Annabel Murray*	3198	0 263 12205 0
A Bewitching Compulsion *Susan Napier*	3199	0 263 12206 9
Hilltop Tryst *Betty Neels*	3200	0 263 12207 7
The Devil's Eden *Elizabeth Power*	3201	0 263 12208 5
Suspicious Heart *Emma Richmond*	3202	0 263 12209 3
Rash Intruder *Angela Wells*	3203	0 263 12210 7

MASQUERADE HISTORICAL ROMANCE

False Fortune *Ann Hulme*	M225	0 263 12361 8
Sapphire in the Snow *Carol Townend*	M226	0 263 12362 6

MEDICAL ROMANCE

Locum Lover *Judith Worthy*	D143	0 263 12359 6
Call an Angel *Hazel Fisher*	D144	0 263 12360 X

LARGE PRINT

Another Man's Ring *Angela Carson*	271	0 263 12059 7
A Bitter Homecoming *Robyn Donald*	272	0 263 12060 0
A Kiss is Still a Kiss *Majorie Lewty*	273	0 263 12061 9
Gentle Deception *Frances Roding*	274	0 263 12062 7
Fire Island *Sally Wentworth*	275	0 263 12064 5
Bridge to Nowhere *Yvonne Whittal*	276	0 263 12064 3
Bond of Destiny *Patricia Wilson*	277	0 263 12065 1
Master of Cashel *Sara Wood*	278	0 263 12066 X

NOVEMBER 1989 HARDBACK TITLES

——— ROMANCE ———

Freeze Frame *Ann Carter*	3204	0 263 12215 8
Pattern of Deceit *Emma Darcy*	3205	0 263 12216 6
Adoring Slave *Rosemary Gibson*	3206	0 263 12217 4
An Arabian Courtship *Lynne Graham*	3207	0 263 12218 2
My Destiny *Rosemary Hammond*	3208	0 263 12219 0
Hazard of Love *Sally Heywood*	3209	0 263 12220 4
Kiss of the Falcon *Stephanie Howard*	3210	0 263 12221 2
Runaway Wife *Charlotte Lamb*	3211	0 263 12222 0
The Seduction of Sara *Joanna Mansell*	3212	0 263 12223 9
Trial by Love *Susanne McCarthy*	3213	0 263 12224 7
The Price of Passion *Elizabeth Oldfield*	3214	0 263 12225 5
Unfriendly Proposition *Jessica Steele*	3215	0 263 12226 3
Steel Tiger *Kay Thorpe*	3216	0 263 12227 1
Snow Demon *Nicola West*	3217	0 263 12228 X
High Heaven *Quinn Wilder*	3218	0 263 12229 8
Threat of Possession *Sara Wood*	3219	0 263 12230 1

MASQUERADE HISTORICAL ROMANCE

Outback Woman *Sally Blake*	M227	0 263 12397 9
Hazardous Marriage *Truda Taylor*	M228	0 263 12398 7

MEDICAL ROMANCE

Accident Prone *Anna Ramsay*	D145	0 263 12395 2
The Human Touch *Grace Read*	D146	0 263 12396 0

LARGE PRINT

Island of the Heart *Sara Craven*	279	0 263 12311 1
A Secure Marriage *Diana Hamilton*	280	0 263 12312 X
Equal Opportunities *Penny Jordan*	281	0 263 12313 8
Dark Mosaic *Anne Mather*	282	0 263 12314 6
The Fateful Bargain *Betty Neels*	283	0 263 12315 4
Unwilling Woman *Sue Peters*	284	0 263 12316 2
Wild Enchantment *Kate Proctor*	285	0 263 12317 0
Friday's Child *Stephanie Wyatt*	286	0 263 12318 9